The Other Rooms

by Jabra Ibrahim Jabra
translated by William Tamplin

DARF PUBLISHERS

Darf Publishers, 2025
277 West End Lane
West Hampstead
London, NW6 1QS

The Other Rooms by Jabra Ibrahim Jabra, translated by William Tamplin

First published as *al-Ghuraf al-ukhra*, Beirut: *al-Mu'assasah al-'arabiyyah li-l-dirasat wa-l-nashr*, 1986

Cover designed by Luke Pajak

ISBN Paperback: 9781850773566
ISBN eBook: 9781850773573

Acknowledgements

For their support of my translation, I'd like to thank Bashir Abu-Manneh, John Cleaver, Sherif Dhaimish, Ghassan Fergiani, Charlie Forrest, Ghazi Gheblawi, Muhammad Fanatil al-Hajaya, Sadeer Jabra, Mika Kasuga, Milbry Polk, Ahmed Saadawi and John Siciliano.

Contents

Foreword

Jabra Ibrahim Jabra is Palestinian literature's most modernizing and experimental novelist. In every one of his six novels – written over four decades, from the 1950s onwards, and in *A World Without Maps* (1982), which he co-authored with Abdul Rahman Munif – Jabra worked to regenerate and transform Arab culture. His work articulated a desire for individual freedom that worked in concert with his striving for social progress and national affirmation. Filled with debate, discussion, challenge, and rebellion, Jabra's novels are unique constructions and are profoundly preoccupied with love and individual redemption as a means of collective change. Indeed, Jabra's stylistic energy was astounding, his discomfort with surrounding Arab society was real, and his modernizing zeal was simply unstoppable.

At every point during his long and productive writing life, Jabra forged new literary forms, tackled contemporary Arab morality and politics, and sought to change the world around him through the medium of art and literary imagination. I can't think of another figure in Arab letters so deeply committed to the value and power of literary and intellectual production—so committed to culture as a resource of challenge and transformation.

What explains Jabra's radical disposition? The short answer is the *nakba*—the Palestinian catastrophe of 1948. As a Palestinian refugee in Baghdad, Jabra understood the *nakba* as not only a national collapse and loss for the Palestinians but also the single most important imperative to modernize the Arab world and to put it on a new footing of national progress and social enlightenment. The answer to the *nakba* wasn't religion, the past, or romantic restoration. The answer lay in a struggle to create a new society that is free, progressive, and oriented toward the future. For Jabra, his cultural intervention would thus be "history-conscious, humanity-conscious and, above all, freedom-conscious."[1]

Jabra's novels, such as *Hunters in a Narrow Street* (1960) and *In Search of Walid Masoud* (1978), are thus defined by the objective to achieve individual and national renewal. He also urged Arab writers, intellectuals, and artists to follow his own generation's pioneering route. As he put it, "I want Arab writers to live with their characters, to struggle with them and argue with them, and through this to participate in depicting at least a part of that overwhelming process: the transformation of our society."[2] Jabra's characters were individual and historical at the same time, defined by a

---

[1] Jabra, "The Rebels and the Committed," in *Celebration of Life: Essays in Literature and Art* (Baghdad: Dar al-Ma'mun, 1988), pp. 59-86, p. 66.

[2] Alaa Elgibali and Barbara Harlow, "Jabra Jabra's Interpoetics: An Interview with Jabra Ibrahim Jabra," *Alif: Journal of Comparative Poetics* (Spring 1981), 49-55 (50).

combination of personal traits and clearly accentuated social values. They were depicted as agents of history, not just as carriers of traditions and structures.

To understand Jabra's trajectory as a writer, as well as his later novels, especially *The Other Rooms* (1986), it is crucial to note that a profound shift takes place in Jabra's writing. At the height of Arab political revolt in the 1960s and 70s, Jabra's novels were realist and constructed narratives of individuals acting in a fundamentally knowable and changeable world. Deeply marked by Palestinian rebellion and Arab hope, Jabra's work presented individual sacrifice as a means of achieving the collective cause of national self-affirmation. Between the late 1970s and the 1980s, Jabra's novels changed in form and substance. Those years shrank the horizons of Palestinian and progressive Arab action, entangled the Palestinians with repressive Arab regimes, corrupted and bureaucratized their vanguard, and led to their political weakening and organizational dispersal after 1982. For Jabra, the civil war in Lebanon stood as a strong anticipatory marker of the worst yet to come.

The Arab world changed in the 1980s. Having seen away the threats of the anti-imperialist nationalist forces of Nasser in Egypt and Qassem in Iraq, oil authoritarianism was back in control, and it began stifling progressive causes in the region. Money, death, and war replaced rebellion, challenge, and hope. This new regressive social order put rebel writers like Jabra on the back foot and undercut their modernizing, emancipatory project. Jabra was left picking up the pieces, with his political hopes crushed by repression and corruption and a profound sense of moral crisis dominating the scene. No longer did individual action seem meaningful, coherent, and conducive to social change. Loss and disorientation now registered their hold on Jabra's world.

Jabra's writing thus went from challenging and changing a world to witnessing its decline and atomization. From hope to siege. This new mode of response is articulated in the following statement, which Jabra made in 1988:

> I shall write to understand why the world besieges me; that is first.
> Secondly, I shall write in the hope of escaping the siege of this world.
> Thirdly, I shall write in the hope of finding, for the whole world, an escape from this siege.

Though these words refer to Jabra's general approach to writing, the statement best speaks to its moment of articulation in the 1980s. The passage could have served as a short preface to Jabra's incredibly powerful novel *The Other Rooms* (1986), as it captures the sense of siege, the role of literature in making sense of it and trying to escape it, and the hope that writing ultimately helps the world overcome that state of siege. What resonates most strongly in *The Other*

Rooms is the novel's sense of suffocation and the defense against conditions that have greatly deteriorated. That is what *The Other Rooms* is fundamentally about.

The Other Rooms is Palestinian literature's most powerful invocation of a degenerative, disintegrative state of individual collapse.[1] Because of that, it is the most pristine articulation of what should be dubbed, in my view, an emerging Palestinian modernism. Its features are universal yet distinctive to Palestinian and Arab conditions. The novel exposes history as nightmare even as it speaks of it, conveys the whirlwind of the existent even as it attempts to shock the reader out of its hold, and captures the liquidation of the self even as it strives and fails to withstand it. In Jabra's insistence on articulating his protagonist's fall, suffering, and withdrawal lies a sliver of utopian redemption. Maybe that is all there is. Maybe that is all that is possible under such conditions of extreme domination. The novel captures this moment, which is nightmarish, disintegrative and yet resistive, all at the same time: it is a unique form that constantly undermines its own claims yet never stops searching for truth or foundations. As such, *The Other Rooms* is a modernist paradigm *par excellence*.

The narrative anchors that were once key for Jabra – a defined city, public-collective commentary, personal history – have become impossible to pin down here. *The Other Rooms*

---

[1] In what follows, I have borrowed liberally from my analysis of the novel in my book *The Palestinian Novel: From 1948 to the Present* (Cambridge: Cambridge University Press, 2016).

is a mockery of the detective elements of, for example, *A World Without Maps.*[1] How can one disentangle causes from effects in a novel that essentially relays an extended nightmare? The reader and protagonist enter a world of unknowing and undecidability. Nothing is what it seems here: knowledge leads to ignorance and more doubt, solidarity to atomized suffering, and reason to unreason.

In a society of total control, where war and Saddam Hussein's security state rule supreme, *The Other Rooms* tries to stand as witness, to make sense of a senseless world of state paranoia and repression. Written in the midst of the utterly senseless Iran-Iraq War, the longest conventional war of the twentieth century, the novel is marked not only by wartime insecurities and state-induced anxieties and control but also by a deep sense of ultimate futility.[2] As in the war, nobody is sure why things happen in the novel or if and how they will ever end. Only suffering is guaranteed. This represents wartime Iraq well. As Eric Davis argues, there was no hiding "the reality that, by the end of the 1980s, the Baathist regime was built on a sectarian and social class base that privileged an increasingly lawless and rapacious elite."[3]

[1] Jabra Ibrahim Jabra, *al-Ghuraf al-ukhra* [*The Other Rooms*] (Beirut: al-Mu'assasah al-'arabiyyah li-l-dirasat wa-l-nashr, 1986).

[2] Salam Abboud describes a "futile war … without results" in *Thaqafat al-'unf fi al-'Iraq* [*The Culture of Violence in Iraq*] (Köln: Al-Kamel, 2002), p. 35.

[3] Eric Davis, *Memories of State: Politics, History, and Collective Identity in Modern Iraq* (Berkeley: University of California Press, 2005), p. 189. Davis concludes that: "The great sacrifices that Iraqis were forced to make during the war with Iran made many realize that, although the regime could offer extensive material benefits, as it had done until 1983, it could also cause tremendous human and material suffering." (p. 199).

Jabra expresses not only his own fears of living under such a brutal yoke but also the human degradation of the Iraqi citizen. The state terror expressed in *The Other Rooms* was real, and intellectuals like Jabra, who chose to remain in an increasingly authoritarian Iraq rather than leave and safeguard their intellectual independence, paid a heavy price. Literature was Jabra's way of naming what he was forced to adapt to: an ideology and practice of political persecution and state tyranny.

The novel's plot is simple. Standing on a city street, the protagonist is whisked off to a compound and moved from one room to another for no evident reason. He keeps meeting the same people, renamed and in disguise. He is also not sure of his own identity, is constantly given different names, and finds himself on a panel being asked to lecture about his critically acclaimed book *The Known and the Unknown*. Along the way, he has erotic encounters with women, is taken to a room full of security files on people, and remains in a state of doubt and confusion: he feels tortured, controlled, and un-free. The suggestion at the end is that the nightmare is actually real and about to begin again. Jabra thus conveys that what the protagonist experiences is not only a state of mind but also a new situation in Baghdad. Unlike all but one of his other novels, *The Other Rooms* ends with 'Baghdad' as the site of authorship, suggesting not only that the novel was written in

Baghdad but also that it is about Baghdad.[1] The nightmare is collective, even as it is experienced by isolated individuals.

The condition Jabra evokes is a kind of oppression that destroys individual agency and collective solidarity. Both are seen to fail in the novel. The individual disintegrates and is crushed by a brutally repressive society, and the collective is a community of sufferers: either spectating *en masse* or waiting for their salvation (sitting in anticipation in front of a door that never opens). If, before, Jabra could utilize individual rebellion and self-sacrifice as a tragic mode of collective redemption, as a trope of connecting the individual with the public, here the disconnect is obvious. The disjuncture is a symptom of the collapse of both entities: individual and collective have been indelibly distorted. It is not only that the public is inactive, but that, like the individual, it has simply disintegrated as an actual and potential agent. An individual bereft of agency and a dazed and un-free collective come face to face and register their hallucinatory atomization. There is no stronger way to convey the shift that has taken place in the Arab world from anticipations of individuals finding their freedom through collective struggle to a condition of all-round crisis and collapse.

The Other Rooms, then, embodies modernism's key artistic distinction. It belongs in the pantheon of universal modernism. Theodor Adorno described modernism's

---

[1] The only exception is *Cry in a Long Night*: "Jerusalem, Summer 1946"

achievements well when he said: "Only through their extreme formal construction do the works of Kafka or Joyce and Beckett become legitimate witnesses to this [extreme historical] horror – reflections on the failure of historical progress."[1] The defeat of Palestinian emancipation and the reconstitution of the Palestinian tragedy – as that of the atomized dispossessed in a repressive Arab world – are very much a part of this twentieth-century horror. Jabra's *The Other Rooms* should thus be read alongside Kafka's, Joyce's, and Beckett's ruminations on human horror that defined the twentieth century.

Bashir Abu-Manneh

---

[1] Peter Hohendahl, *Prismatic Thought: Theodor W. Adorno* (Lincoln: University of Nebraska Press, 1995), p. 87.

On Jabra Ibrahim Jabra

I.

When I was nearing the end of high school in the late 1980s, I first came across a novel by Jabra Ibrahim Jabra: *Hunters in a Narrow Street*. Jabra had originally written it in English. It was published in 1960 and later translated into Arabic. I had already gained a wide familiarity with Iraqi novels, most of which didn't interest me because of their experimental feel and the obscurity of the storylines. In the late 1980s, this was understandable on account of the authoritarian regime of Saddam Hussein. Writers avoided directness and any sort of commentary on political or social issues.

In Jabra's novel, I found what was missing in the Iraqi novels I'd read up until then: Iraq. From the perspective of a foreign observer – the Palestinian protagonist Jameel Farran – *Hunters in a Narrow Street* penetrates the depths, shades and practices of Iraqi life. I believe it was the first novel, Iraqi or Arab, to portray a Shiite mourning ritual. By the late 1980s, delving into such details was politically off-limits for writers. Despite my knowledge that the novel had been written in the late 1950s, and even though I was reading it in the late 1980s, it was charged with an extraordinary and lively precision. It was fresh and inviting, as if it had been written yesterday.

In the years following my initial acquaintance with Jabra's work, I read the rest of his novels. I can't claim that *The Other Rooms* had a particular role in the formation of my literary character. Yet with his broad experience, Jabra was the writer who influenced me most. It might be said that because of him and Abdul Rahman Munif, my desire to become a novelist strengthened and solidified during my young adulthood. (I never once saw Munif, but I may have crossed paths with Jabra when I was a university student as he roamed the halls and auditoriums of the best-known arts center in Baghdad, the Saddam Center for the Arts, in the company of other writers and artists.)

Beginning in the 1940s, Jabra Ibrahim Jabra lived through the vicissitudes of Iraqi cultural, social and political history. He was both a close friend to, and a collaborator with, the most prominent Iraqi writers and poets, such as Badr Shakir al-Sayyab, a pioneer of modern Arabic poetry. It's well established that Jabra influenced Sayyab. He helped him gain familiarity with ancient myths and employ them in his poetry after Jabra translated portions of Sir James Frazer's *The Golden Bough*. Indeed, Jabra's critical approach to art, poetry and the novel left a pronounced mark on the Iraqi cultural scene. He produced advanced models of the Arabic novel that contained his adventurousness and experimentation and that were more sophisticated than other Arab novels of the era. As a writer of modern Arabic novels, Jabra is first-class. In *The Other Rooms*, Jabra pursued his sense of literary adventure to the furthest reaches of alienation. For that reason, this novel stands alone among his *oeuvre* and serves as an early example of Arabic literature's employment of alienation.

Along with Abdul Rahman Munif, Jabra was the most influential writer in the formation of my literary personality. It was a refreshing and unexpected shot of life when I got ahold of the novel Jabra and Munif wrote together, *A World Without Maps*—for there were my two favorite writers weaving a shared text. Munif was half-Saudi, half-Iraqi, and perhaps also half-Jordanian, if you'll permit the math. In addition to Munif and Jabra, Ghassan Kanafani and Mahmoud Darwish also influenced my literary formation. By coincidence, the last three are all Palestinians. But there was something special about Jabra: he's not fully Palestinian, and neither is he fully Iraqi. Jabra combined numerous identities and simultaneously transcended their boundaries. His Palestinian nature remained powerfully present at the heart of his literary production. After all, most of his protagonists are Palestinians. Yet Jabra lived in Iraq, became an Iraqi citizen, and not only married an Iraqi woman but also converted from Syriac Orthodox Christianity to Islam. It was on the Iraqi scene that Jabra broke out into the larger public sphere – academic, literary and cultural – and it was from Iraq that Jabra's name went forth into other Arab regions, and from there to the world.

There's another side to Jabra's variegated identity, and that is his wide array of interests. He was a novelist, poet, painter, art critic, translator, and literary critic. Jabra's trajectory accompanied the beginnings of the Iraqi modernist movement in literature and art. He was a great influence on the pioneers of art, poetry and the novel in Iraq, and he was in turn influenced by them. Jabra was, with his varied literary and cultural identity, a crucial player in Iraqi modernism. The variety of Jabra's interests represents a personal connection between him and me, for he was, from the very beginning of his literary and artistic production, a likeness of me, yet magnified. Like Jabra, I am a painter and a poet, and I too write stories and novels. At a later stage in my life, when I was at university, I faced down my friends and colleagues – who would criticize the diversity of my interests – by invoking the name of Jabra Ibrahim Jabra: the writer, the artist, the translator and the poet who excelled in all he put his hand to.

II.

Jabra produced more than twelve works of narrative, including novels, short story collections and autobiographies. Every one of those works won the interest of critics and the engagement of readers. Jabra kept pace with the literary currents of the day, with which he had a comprehensive familiarity through his mastery of English. In addition, Jabra was one of the new literary voices in the Arab world. These voices appeared in the 1960s and sought to distance themselves from the experience of the "pioneering generation," which busied itself with the social realist novel and was represented most prominently by Naguib Mahfouz.

The Arabic Novel of the Sixties witnessed the snake-oil enchantments that accompanied the rise of Arab nationalism, the convulsions that followed its grandiose promises, the Arabs' defeat by Israel, and the disaster that befell the Palestinians. We find the clearest echo of all that in the works of Palestinian writers such as Jabra Ibrahim Jabra. The collapse of expansive visions of the future, the betrayal of the political and social hero, and the entry into a world of barrenness, absurdity and meaninglessness—all those were themes that converged in the literary production of that generation. We see this in the disappearance of Walid Masoud, the absent protagonist in Jabra's novel *In Search of Walid Masoud*. We see the same in Jabra's novel *The Journals of Sarab Affan*, in which despair overwhelms the author's political frame of reference, and in which the dream of returning to Palestine becomes a mirage—the Arabic for which is *sarab*, the name of the novel's female protagonist. In his novel *The Ship*, we find Jabra aspiring to connect with the Western modernist novel in his employment of the multiple-narrator technique, popularized by William Faulkner. Jabra translated Faulkner's most famous novel, *The Sound and the Fury*, into Arabic.

21

In the novel that Jabra co-wrote with Abdul Rahman Munif, *A World Without Maps*, we see those writers' adventurous spirit emerge as they plunge into a shared experience. Co-writing is rare in modern Arabic literature, even though I suspect that Jabra's imprint looms larger over the novel than Munif's. Adventure is on display in other elements of *A World Without Maps*, as well, in the writers' invention of the imaginary city of Amouriya, which takes its features from manifold cities in the modern Arab world. We also see here an echo of Faulkner's imaginary milieu in the American South – Yoknapatawpha County. In *A World Without Maps*, we see the classic Jabran themes of wandering, alienation, and the loss of meaning, as well as echoes of the political situation, the theme of resistance, the Palestinian cause, and feelings of bitterness that followed Arab defeats.

In all his novels, Jabra was keen to mix his wide intellectual and artistic knowledge with the narratives' dramatic events. He was also keen to tap into his own personality and elements of his memoirs and autobiographies to build the characters and backstories of his protagonists. In Jabra's able hands, the novel is not just a lyrical monologue of the protagonist but a sociological and cultural study, a vast record that reflects the diversity of Jabra's sources of knowledge even as it reflects the diversity of his literary and artistic preoccupations that found, in the novel, the greatest expanse in which to roam.

III.

Jabra published *The Other Rooms* in 1986 with the Arab Institute for Research and Publishing in Beirut, Lebanon. But the last page of the novel notes the place of its composition: Baghdad. We don't have precise details on the history of its composition, but we can assume that it was written in 1985 or slightly before that. Those years saw the climax of the Iran-Iraq War. The following year, 1986, witnessed a devastating military defeat for Iraq: the loss of the Faw peninsula after it was conquered by the Iranian army. Located south of Basra, the Faw is Iraq's single point of entry into the Persian Gulf and is a key port for oil export.

In those days, the atmosphere in Iraq was suffused with the stench of blood, smoke and battles on the front line. Yet the one official TV channel available to Iraqis played songs about victory and heroism, songs that glorified the "wise leadership" of President Saddam Hussein. Moreover, Iraqi state television was in the business of advertising official cultural activities, yearly festivals concerned with poetry such as the Mirbad Festival. The Mirbad Festival effectively revived the classical Arabian ode, against which modernist Arab poets had rebelled. This kind of poem was appropriate for occasions of praise, and Saddam and his Baath party posse understood it far better than they did the cryptic works that young writers were producing at the time. These cultural activities and festivals, on which the state spent vast sums of money, hosted Arab writers and the leading lights of poetry and culture. Many of them were compelled to glorify the greatness of the president's wise leadership and his acts of heroism on the war's front line. Some chose to.

On the sidelines of this deluge of propagandistic literature and art dedicated to the glorification of Saddam, more refined literature and art were maturing and announcing themselves. You could even say that they represented a kind of health in Iraqi culture. Any writer who wanted to maintain a coherent ethical position would find himself walking a tightrope with isolation on the one side and the wrath of the ruling authorities on the other. Angering them meant the possibility of harsh punishment that sometimes led to death, as happened with Aziz al-Sayed Jassem. Despite Jassem's nationalistic political leanings that jibed with those of the regime, he was imprisoned twice. The second time, in 1991, he died in prison. Or he was neutralized, if we believe his brother, the professor and critic Muhsin al-Musawi. The same thing happened to the famous singer Sabah al-Sahl, who was imprisoned for verbally attacking the president. He was executed in 1993.

In those days, Jabra existed at the beating heart of Iraqi cultural life as a refined critic, a well-known writer, and a mentor to young writers. (He believed that there was always something new that young writers were capable of bringing forth in every age.) In his work, Jabra flitted between the various cultural institutions of the Iraqi state

24

and was close friends with many of the regime's cultural bigwigs. He was compelled to engage in writing, for money, propagandistic literature mobilized to support the war and to give statements in Iraqi newspapers that praised the president's "wise leadership." Yet Jabra never went very far in his "support," as did many Iraqi writers and others from around the Arab world. He took shelter in his own private ivory tower from the dangers of being turned into a mouthpiece of propaganda for Saddam Hussein's regime.

In his ivory tower, Jabra could move among the upper floors of Iraqi life, far from the raucous fray and the oppressive conditions of discourse on the street. There on the uppermost floors, Jabra was preoccupied with the modern currents of visual art, with theorizing and critiquing modern poetry—poetry that didn't serve the propagandistic needs of the regime, for it was an elite kind of poetry, obscure at times, and concerned with universal, indirect topics. In *The Other Rooms*, Jabra was not concerned with examining the Iraqi social, cultural and political scene with any precision, even if he did draw from it in building some of his themes and characters. There are critics who indicated early on – and perhaps because of this he was accused of residing in an ivory tower – that Jabra avoided direct reference to political topics and themes. The Iraqi critic Fatema al-Muhsin, for example, points out not only that Jabra, in his critical readings of literary and artistic works, ignored their hidden political aspects but also that he avoided talking about writers who broke with the ruling regime, one example of whom was Saadi Youssef.

Later on, I came to reinterpret aspects of Jabra's experience and ended up writing on him – and his "ivory tower" – in the literary press. Perhaps he wasn't emblematic of an ivory tower but of an ambivalent eye, doubly charged, both separate from and integrated with the world it observed. Perhaps that ivory tower was more like a well-lit stage for the events and personalities about which the author wrote, as the English novelist and critic John Braine once suggested. Even in his work that displays the most alienation, *The Other Rooms*, we perceive the work as separate from its environment for artistic reasons and, at the same time, integrated with the world it's speaking about. All the events are radiantly apparent and do not drown in sophistry, linguistic games, or highfalutin obfuscations. The literary characteristics embodied in Jabra's experience with fiction later prevailed, becoming commonplace in Arabic fiction.

Jabra continued to walk the line between the deluge of political events, news of the merciless war and the tragedies along the front lines, and the whirlpool of his own personal feelings of alienation, like a "hunter in a narrow alley," as Fatema al-Muhsin put it, riffing on the title of Jabra's 1960 novel. Even the date of Jabra's death – only two years after the death of his Iraqi wife Lami'ah al-Askari (for whom he changed his religion, though not for intellectual or theological reasons) – was during the worst of times in Iraq: 1994, when the weight of international sanctions on Iraq had turned the country into a large, nightmarish prison.

IV.

Many readers of *The Other Rooms* will not be able to stop themselves, while reading, from examining the reality, the country, and the city in which the novel was written and whose name the author recorded at the novel's end: Baghdad. This was the Baghdad that existed during the abattoir of the horrific war and the rule of an authoritarian regime. This was the Baghdad in which the state's security services curbed the right to free expression, the right to write freely. The reader will understand, from between the lines of the novel, something that the author wanted to say indirectly, and that is a particular sentence on page 58 of the Arabic edition: "Our true opinions spring from within and flow back in again." Or the protagonist's speech on page 77, when he shouts at the attendants of a strange dinner party held in his honor: "Nowadays, ladies and gentlemen, our nights are choked with blood. Behind that large door of yours, behind its two lofty panels, corpses are accumulating."

Corpses really were accumulating in those days. Iraq had been put on the defensive after it lost swathes of territory to the Iranians' human-wave attacks, in which young Iranian men were pushed to the front, driven by death and inspired by suicide in such a way that, back then at least, confounded

Iraqis. Due to the mounting casualties, the Iraqi regime recruited men – retirees and those exempt from military service for health reasons or because they held civilian jobs – and jumbled them together into a new creation called "The Popular Army."

Azzam Spinks' blathering in *The Other Rooms* reminds me of the nonsense spewed by the Baathist Party's "intellectuals," who composed hundreds of meaningless newspaper articles that glorified the regime with their glistening prose. And let's remember that Spinks' Arabic last name, Abu al-Hor, is fashioned from the Iraqi noun *hor*, which is not in use in other Arabic dialects. The word means "marsh" and refers to the riverine marshes for which Iraq is famous. It was as if Jabra wanted to link the nonsense Spinks was spewing with a specifically Iraqi character who represented an aspect of authority and hegemony over the peculiar environment in which the novel's hero finds himself besieged and imprisoned.

It was as if the hero here is a representation of Jabra, forced to go along with the official nonsense that surrounded him in his places of work within the state's cultural institutions. It's as if he's imprisoned along with his jailers, who, even though they're his jailers, interact with him in a spirit of friendship and goodwill. The character Abu al-Hor – "Spinks" in the English translation, from its proximity to "Abu al-Hol," which means "Sphinx" – acts this way toward the protagonist. And let's recall that the name of the character "Alewi" is quintessentially Iraqi, a diminutive and affectionate form of the name "Ali." Like the word *hor*, it's not used in any other Arabic dialects.

Moreover, on page 35 of the novel's Arabic edition, we read:

I turned toward the television. With great boredom and impatience, I pressed the ON button. A crowd was clapping for a man addressing them from a stage. I turned the sound dial up to hear what he was saying. Damn! It was broken, so I was left with just a silent picture of a man talking excitedly, his hands moving ceaselessly, a crowd interrupting him with its applause...

To any Iraqi who lived through that era, the scene will remind them of routine daily occurrences that many Iraqis followed on Iraqi television. Those days featured many podiums and daises, many stages and pulpits, many people reciting popular poetry glorifying the regime and the war. And there were always storms of applause.

Not only that—Saddam would take up hours of the daily broadcast to hold forth, spouting maxims and proverbs to his audience of party members and military leaders. Many of these proverbs were edited and revised to become polished and refined Arabic phrases published in the next day's newspapers. In subsequent years, little booklets appeared carrying "The Sayings of the Leader," some of which made their way into school curriculums. Students were forced to memorize them and were tested on them.

Did Jabra, in writing this novel, run the risk of angering his friends who counted themselves among the regime's intellectuals and who could well understand his symbols and literary references? The text of the novel does not actually offer strong, reliable evidence that would make my preceding interpretations of it sound and well-documented. Yet we could argue that Jabra was certainly smarter than his colleagues among the regime's intellectuals. And they were present in his mind as he wrote—as were his readers. In the nooks and crannies of his prose, Jabra said what he wanted to say. He expressed those "true opinions [that] spring from within and flow back in again" without direct reference to the actual state of affairs in Iraq.

The hero is in over his head. He has forgotten his name and, during the events of the novel, he assumes many names. At times he is Nimr Alwan, and at others he is Adel al-Tibi. In the final pages of the novel, he adopts a new one: Fares al-Saqqar. The hero is lost in a labyrinth that resembles the one in the novel *Djinn* by Alain Robbe-Grillet. Had Jabra read that novel? It came out in French in 1981 and then in English the following year. Jabra was an attentive follower of the English-language literary scene, but we do not know for certain that he read it. Certain scholars are given to comparing the atmosphere of *The Other Rooms* with *The Trial* by Franz Kafka, one of the Western authors most widely read in the Arab world. And there's no doubt that Kafka influenced many Arab writers' styles and approaches.

In any event, the protagonist's actions and his responses
to the events in *The Other Rooms* make him seem like a sleep-
walker or someone living in a nightmare. He doesn't offer
much resistance, and he sometimes prefers to go along with
whatever is happening around him in order to discover the
next step. The events occur during a single night, in an
undefined place, and in an unknown city and country with
no landmarks or distinguishing features that could help define
the identity of either. The other characters, male and female,
manipulate him and his nerves. But they don't humiliate him
or torture him, instead treating him with respect and plunging
with him into prolonged conversations that mainly consist
of meaningless, elegant nonsense. Nimr, or Adel, inhabits a
vortex in which he's moved from one room to another. Yet
he doesn't perceive a serious threat to his life, and it seems
that a profound serenity shines down on the hero's words
and deeds, as happens to us during sleep. Even in the most
terrifying dreams, there exists the feeling that awakening will
put an end to the threat.

V.

Jabra published *The Other Rooms* four years after his shared
project with Abdul Rahman Munif, *A World Without Maps*.
Perhaps Jabra remained in that world "without maps" when
he began working on *The Other Rooms*, for this is a novel that
also occurs in a mapless world. Jabra may be urging the

reader to ask this question: If the novel's protagonist is lost and confused inside the interconnected other rooms, then which room is the first room, the room that the hero doesn't perceive as "other"? It might be that room in which the novel's hero—or author—can express with ease and serenity those private opinions that "spring from within and flow back in again."

The hero of *The Other Rooms* emerges from his labyrinth and greets the light of a new day. But his companion informs him that they are embarking on another round, another meeting with an audience the hero doesn't recognize, and that he will again be compelled to lecture on his book, *The Known and the Unknown*. Yet now the hero appears relaxed. He doesn't resist the partial amnesia in which he lives, and neither does he resist being forced to plunge into yet another labyrinth. It is as if the nightmarish life of the labyrinth has become a lifestyle. Throughout many eras, and up until now, Iraqis have come to understand the labyrinth-as-lifestyle better than anyone else.

by Ahmed Saadawi
translated by William Tamplin

The Other Rooms

An old story tells of a prince who fell madly in love with a woman from among the commoners. He married her. Out of the intensity of his love, he set aside for her, and for her alone, an old palace he had inherited from his father and in which he took great pride. The day he settled her in the palace, he informed her that it contained forty rooms, thirty-nine of which she could use. Each room was full to bursting with Persian rugs, opulent furnishings, and precious stones. But the fortieth room was not for her; it was forbidden. And the wife appeared content. Yet whenever she went wandering and frolicking all throughout the palace and its thirty-nine rooms, she continued to burn with curiosity, with the desire to enter the other room, the fortieth room.

One day the prince went out hunting and had most of the palace's servants and retainers accompany him. Seizing the opportunity of their absence, his wife went to the door of the forbidden room with a box full of the palace's keys. She began trying them in the door's lock, one by one. Yet she failed to open the lock, and the door remained shut.

She didn't hesitate before rushing off to a servant's room to return with a large hammer that she could barely wield. With all the strength she could muster, she raised it, brought it crashing down upon the door, and broke it to pieces.

She entered the room, and—lo and behold!—it branched out into interconnecting rooms, and each room ramified, in its turn, into yet more rooms. She heard a voice telling her, 'If that is indeed you, princess, then turn back now, before you regret it! Otherwise, you won't leave here as you've come!' She said, 'Dear God, how did the voice know I was a princess? That must have been the voice of the Devil!' And she refused to heed the advice she heard.

***

There's another version of this story that holds that the prince's wife, when taking advantage of her day alone, went to the door of the forbidden room with the box full of keys. She had hardly tried the first key when she discovered that the door wasn't even locked. Indeed, it swung open as soon as she laid her hand upon it, as if it had been waiting for her. And she entered the room…

Chapter One

The plaza was one of the city's main squares. Along one side of it stretched a dense row of eucalyptus trees. Tall buildings, standing close on each other, occupied the other three sides. It was a lonesome square at that hour. Not a soul moved, either within the square or along its edges. No car or any other kind of vehicle passed through it. The time? Not afternoon exactly, but after sundown, just before darkness falls, in those lonesome, anxious moments that have wearied of the day and begun to yearn for a night slow in coming. The remaining daylight was leaden, dusty, and imbued with failure and sadness. And the wide square was empty, forlorn, abandoned, forsaken by God and man, as if the city no longer contained anyone to move within it, to strive, to love — as if a plague had swept over it and spared no one.

On the sidewalk I stood next to a man I didn't recognize. I didn't quite know what had brought us together. We stood there, silent, gazing at the trees in the little copse opposite us. Every now and then we turned our gazes this way or that, waiting for something. Suddenly, the sounds of automatic gunfire peppered out from between the trees. I was amazed to see thousands of birds shooting forth like shards from the tree branches and growing more and more distant in the sky. Then silence returned. My companion, wearing an old black coat that reached his ankles, muttered, 'Even the birds...' I didn't know whether he'd said that to me or to himself. But he looked at me, clearly expecting a response. I didn't move, and I didn't say anything as my eyes followed the birds in their surprised, random flight until they disappeared.

The man didn't give up trying to win me over. He took out a pack of cigarettes and offered me one, but I shook my head without uttering a word. He stuck one between his lips, lit it with a lighter, and exhaled the smoke from his mouth with a grumble of displeasure and what resembled a hiss.

From afar I heard the rumble of a car approaching from our right. My gaze drifted toward the road I expected the car to emerge from. From the magnitude of the sound, I guessed it would be a large truck. And indeed, a truck entered the square. Behind the cab, a green tarpaulin covered the bed. The truck was speeding down the other side of the square, alongside the trees, so I raised my hand to hail the driver, and the man standing near me followed suit. Indeed, he waved his arm with a surfeit of excitement and yelled: 'Here! Here!'

The driver saw us and slowed down a bit. Then he turned in our direction and drove until he reached us, coming to a complete stop. I saw that the truck was open from the back and that its bed was full of people. Thirty or forty men and women stood there under the tarp. When the truck stopped, they fell into each other, but because there were so many of them, they remained standing, crammed together. And strangely silent.

My companion walked toward the tailgate, pushed open the bolt on the right and then the one on the left, and lowered it. He went up on the truck bed to join the passengers as they gazed at him with indifference. When I didn't follow his lead, but instead continued to scrutinize their faces to see if I could recognize any of them, the leaden gloom not helping me very much, a man's voice arose between them. 'Get moving!' he said. 'Aren't you getting on?'

'Who are you all?' I asked.

A young woman standing near the edge laughed quasi-hysterically. 'He wants to know who we are!' she said. Then she turned to me defiantly. 'And why, sir, do you wish to know who we are?'

Just as I was astonished to see the birds shoot forth in flocks from the trees upon hearing the gunfire, I was likewise astonished when that young woman turned her back to me, lifted high the hems of her skirt to expose her bare buttocks, and began shaking them shamelessly before my eyes. At that moment, several people next to her bent over to raise the tailgate and bolted it shut, the young woman continuing to display her round white buttocks before me. Then she pulled her skirt down, turned back around to face me, and leaned over to rest on the low-slung tailgate. 'There's no one left who hasn't gotten on with us,' she said. 'Come on up.'

'Get in, man!' said a loud voice from the depths of the truck. 'Don't make us late!'

I focused my gaze on them again, but I couldn't distinguish a single face I recognized. In fact, I don't believe I saw faces, at least according to the commonly accepted meaning of that word but, rather, dozens of masks, obscure and indistinct. Except, that is, for the face of the young woman who'd bestowed her wantonness upon me, and her invitation. It was a youthful face not entirely devoid of beauty and surrounded by coal-black hair that reached her shoulders, strands of which were matted and strewn over her forehead and cheeks: a face I didn't recognize, but one I could perceive with clarity.

I shook my head and said nothing. I'd hardly retreated to the sidewalk when the truck roared to life, turned around in the square, and shot off noisily in its former direction. I followed it with my eyes as it drew farther and farther away down the long road before fading away entirely.

Then I felt terribly lonely. I almost regretted my refusal to board the truck, but again I convinced myself of the need to wait until I saw someone I knew or was comfortable around. I wonder where they're going? I asked myself. And who are they? Why did my companion join them with such speed and enthusiasm?

Suddenly the streetlights around the square were illuminated, as were those on either side of the road. But what caught my eye was that not a single light shone in the windows of the buildings around me, all of which were multi-storied.

I paced back and forth on the sidewalk, anxious and stressed with anticipation. Yet I didn't know whom or what I was anticipating. 'One can't live with such forgetfulness,' I said. 'No way!'

When I saw someone approaching from afar, walking slowly toward me on the deserted sidewalk, I thought it might be a man I knew. I couldn't make out his face – he'd turned up the collar of his raincoat so that it covered his chin and jawline, and his hands were planted in his pockets – until he got very close to me. I thought he would take the initiative and greet me, but he continued on his slow walk. He passed me by without so much as a turn toward me, without even the furtive glance of a passing stranger. For a moment it occurred to me that I recognized his face, but I was wrong. I suppressed the desire to stop him and speak with him. Instead, I continued to let my gaze follow him as he walked off. When he'd gone past me about twenty or thirty meters, he stopped. He turned in place like someone checking his whereabouts. I continued to watch him. For a few minutes, he didn't move. Afterwards, he resumed walking and moved on until I saw him turn down a side street and disappear.

For all my preoccupation with the man, it turned out that I'd failed to notice a car approaching me from behind. That is, until the sound of its engine grew louder and caused me to spin around. With its lights turned off, the car crept along and pulled to a stop beside me. 'Ah, thank God, finally!' I told myself. Through the window, I fixed my gaze on the driver and saw that it was a woman. She turned on the car's interior lights so I could see her better.

'Excuse me,' she said from behind the wheel, 'have you seen a man in a raincoat pass this way?'

'Yes,' I said.

'When?'

'A few minutes ago.'

'Where did he go?'

'He went down that side street. The second one on the right.'

'Thank you,' she said. But she didn't move. She kept staring at me. 'Were you waiting for me?' she asked.

I wasn't lying when I replied, 'I really don't know.'

She laughed with a pure, clear voice. 'Of course you were waiting for me,' she said. 'Come on, get in here beside me.'

Without hesitation, I opened the door, got into the car, and sat down next to her. I had the feeling I'd been spared the distress of anticipation and boredom. As soon as I'd settled in my seat and begun scrutinizing her face as she put the car in first gear, I realized that her face wasn't new to me. 'Didn't I see you about half an hour ago?' I asked her.

'You saw me? Where?'

'In the truck, with a bunch of men and women.'

'What truck?'

'A truck that passed by here a while ago. You were standing near the back of it, near the tailgate.'

'What are you talking about?'

'You turned your back to me and raised the hem of your skirt...'

'Me?'

'You yourself! And you wanted me to join you.'

She didn't reply. I noticed that she'd passed the side street down which the man with the raincoat had turned. She didn't turn down it but instead continued down the main drag. 'Have you changed your mind about the man in the raincoat?' I asked.

'The man I asked you about? He doesn't matter to me one bit.'

'Then why did you ask me about him?'

'Just feminine curiosity, nothing more.'

In the silence that settled between us for a few minutes, I was sure she was the young woman who'd asked me to board the truck. I hadn't forgotten how she'd worn her black hair, which reached her shoulders, strands of which were strewn over her forehead. When I lowered my eyes to her skirt – despite the darkness that had begun to fill the car – I was sure, and I don't know how, that it was the same skirt she'd raised over her behind with such weird wantonness in the truck. Yet I, with my ill luck, couldn't remember the skirt's color. What kind of trap had I landed myself in?

Until then, the young lady hadn't turned on the headlights, relying instead on streetlights to light her way. 'Why don't you turn on the headlights?' I asked her.

She turned to me, astonished. 'But why? The streets are all empty.'

'Aren't you afraid of an accident, or an emergency of some sort?'

'Not at all. I know this road like the back of my hand.'

A bold thought crossed my mind. 'Look,' I said, 'if you'd permit me, could I just lift up this skirt of yours?'

'While I'm driving?'

'Just to make sure of something.'

'Which is?'

'To see if you're wearing anything under it.'

She burst out laughing as she clung to the wheel. 'Are you crazy?' she asked. 'Or do you think *I* am?'

'I just want to make sure you were the young lady I saw in the truck. That's all there is to it.'

I was happy when she made a strange movement with her right leg, which she was using for the gas pedal. She raised her knee in my direction and with a touch of nervousness, said, 'Go ahead, lift my skirt up, just as you like.'

With a quasi-automatic reflex, I reached my hand toward her knee before she could re-situate it to continue driving. I took hold of the skirt's hem. But then my fingers settled on her knee and didn't move. I suppressed my shameful desire to stroke her leg and withdrew my hand. 'I beg your pardon,' I said. 'What are you going to think of me? I'm sorry for my behavior.'

'No, not at all. Uncertainty's bothersome. I should know.'

'And worrisome.'

'But don't you want to remain in just a bit of doubt?' she asked.

'I prefer to know the truth if I can.'

'Which truth?'

'Ah... Knowable truth, at the very least,' I said.

She laughed with a derision that, I won't deny, I found attractive. 'A small ask!' she said. 'Of course, there's also truth that's unknowable. But let's assume that in your attempt to do away with doubt, you discovered something you hadn't taken into consideration.'

I wasn't in a mental state fit for such intellectual conversation, and with a strange woman whose name I didn't even know. I continued to focus my gaze on the long road ahead, illuminated on both sides and empty of people and cars. My hostess wasn't satisfied with my silence. 'You didn't answer my question,' she added.

'What question?'

'You're trying to use certainty to get rid of your doubt. And that's all fine and good. But what if, in the process, you discovered a truth that wasn't the one you were looking for?'

'The matter would then depend on the truth that I discovered,' I said with a touch of despair. 'That doesn't mean I would be through with the old doubt,' I added. 'The new truth wouldn't necessarily remove the old doubt. Worry is as old as dirt. So is bother.'

'And if you found that the truth you incidentally discovered also caused you worry and bother?'

'Don't complicate things. Please.'

'It seems you think remaining in doubt is, in itself, worrisome. And that truth, whatever it may be, removes worry – in so far as truth is beauty, and beauty is... Or am I putting words into your mouth—'

'Yes. You're putting words into my mouth that aren't even in my head.'

'I'm sorry.'

'But, as you said. Truth, whatever it may be... Ugh! What is it you want from this sophistry? Was I really waiting for you? Why did you ask me to ride with you?'

'I see that you're upset. That's all right. You can get out wherever you want. Here, for instance?'

She braked a little too sharply and brought the car to a halt. She turned to me with a great deal of defiance that I could distinguish even in the darkness of the car. The streetlights cast a bit of wan light on her face, and I saw two points gleaming in her eyes amid two pools of black. I hadn't been upset, as she'd claimed, but her braking so abruptly did upset me. Things only got worse when she turned on the car's interior lights as if she wanted me to see with my own two eyes how serious she was in her position. Dear God! Here was a beautiful woman who'd come to me from I knew not where. How could I leave her so easily? Did I have to leave her? And where would I get out on this long, desolate path that ended in some unknown place?

I didn't reply. And I didn't move for several moments as she gazed into my eyes. With my right hand I reached for the door handle and opened it slightly. But I shut it again, violently. 'I don't want to get out,' I said.

'Shall I continue then?'

'Yes, continue.'

'Excellent!'

'But, where to?'

She raised her hand to the car's interior light and turned it off. Then she put the car in gear. 'You'll see,' she said laconically.

Then I returned my focus to the road, perhaps to glimpse a landmark so I could orient myself. I was a native son of this city, and I knew it street by street. No—yard by yard. And now it terrified me to realize that I didn't know my own city. My eyes didn't alight on a single building I recognized. But perhaps there hadn't been buildings here before. Even when my driver finally turned on the headlights, I didn't see anything I recognized save a circular logo with three radii inside it, raised just above the hood of the car, which alerted me to the fact that it was a Mercedes-Benz. Apart from the regularity of the streetlights, only the darkness appeared on either side of us. As if we were shooting forth into the desert. Or perhaps along the seashore. No, we were no longer in the city. We were far from the city, absolutely. Perhaps we were on the highway between one city and another. My chauffeuse appeared totally confident in herself and her driving, reassured that she was rushing through a wilderness I was unfamiliar with but that she knew down to the last detail.

A few minutes passed during which I surrendered to reality. I lowered the window to revive myself with the cool, moist air that began beating against my face. The young woman must have noticed me withdraw my attention. It was usually within my power to absent myself completely from my surroundings when necessary, as if my mind contained a deep cave into which I could crawl and not hear or see anyone. In that deep cave of mine, I now began relishing the cool, moist air beating against my face and hearing music I'd been fond of listening to in the past few days—Chopin's *Nocturnes*. They were part of my internal defense against the slings and arrows of daily life. I would imagine Chopin the youth as he left the bed of his lover, George Sand, in the darkness of Mallorca, while rain noisily pelted the deserted island and, in the rooms of the old house, felt his way by the light of a candle to the piano that would with its melodies free him from all that beset him, that would liberate him from his malady and woes, if only for another night.

I was stunned when the young lady scolded me. 'How many times have I told you to close the window!' she yelled. 'Can't you hear? Aren't you cold enough? I'll turn the music off, just to punish you.'

I realized she was playing a cassette tape in the car's stereo. She flicked it off with a nervous gesture of her finger. 'Was that *you* playing the Chopin?' I asked her with a voice full of confusion as I closed the window.

'What do you think? Was that *you* playing it?'

'But that cassette...'

'What about it?'

'It's from my collection.'

'Oh really? You crack me up—as if you're the only one who buys cassette tapes.'

'Do you have any others?'

'I have dozens. When we get there, you can look through all of them.'

'Get there? Where?'

'You'll see.'

'*You'll see, you'll see!* Why don't you tell me who you are? Where are you taking me on this endless road?'

'We'll get there soon.'

'I'm sure we will.'

'You don't believe me? Do you think I'll keep driving you around in this car till the morning comes?'

'Why wouldn't you? Anything's possible in this life.'

Again she let out a sweet, derisive laugh from her limpic throat as if she weren't my jailer but my friend. In a tone closer to coquetry, she said, 'You, as a doctor, would know better than anyone else. Right?'

With her right hand she patted me gently on the thigh to reassure me. Or was it to feel me up? Because she kept her hand there. I, however, was determined not to respond.

And I was overtaken by the powerful suspicion that she was playing a game of cat and mouse with me. I told myself that, if she intended to devour me, then may she do so in one gulp. There was no need for this ridiculous manipulation.

I didn't say anything. I wanted to crawl back down to my deep internal cave to erase her presence, even for a few minutes. But she turned her head toward me, her hand still resting on my thigh. 'Don't you smoke?' she asked.

I was slow in answering: 'I do. Sometimes.'

'Then light me a cigarette.'

I produced a pack of cigarettes from my pocket, took one out, and offered it to her silently without taking one for myself. She took it from me only to return it, saying in a tone mixed with coquetry and command: 'Light it, then give it to me.'

She pointed at the car's cigarette lighter and pressed it while I put the pack between us as if to say: *Feel free to smoke more whenever you like.*

I pulled out the car's lighter and lit the cigarette with a bit of nervous tension. Then I took it from my lips and offered it to her. She took it and placed it between hers. 'And now, light yourself one too,' she said.

I shook my head sharply. 'I don't feel like smoking.'

She took the cigarette between two of her fingers. 'I get it,' she said. 'You're refusing. No problem.'

She pulled out the ashtray, stubbed out her cigarette, and

slammed it shut. I reveled in her anger and refocused my eyes on the road without saying a word.

This time it didn't take us long. We reached a turn-off on the left, which we took a little too sharply, such that the car's wheels screeched keenly. The road here was much narrower than the one we'd been on. After a while we turned left again and entered a road as narrow as an alley. It was an unlit road with trees arranged in an orderly fashion on either side. And it was only a few minutes before we came to a wide, open plot of land. The car's headlights illuminated a large, multi-storey house standing on one side of it. We'd hardly glimpsed it when its windows lit up.

The young lady parked near the house. 'Go on, get out,' she said after her long bout of silence.

We both got out. Suddenly I saw a huge truck approaching us from the opposite side. And I screamed – yes, I screamed like a madman, 'No! No!'

But the young lady said, rather indifferently, as if dealing with a naughty child, 'Stop yelling. Stop yelling, please!'

'But this is the truck I saw in the square—back there...'

'And why wouldn't it be?'

'What do you want from me?' I screamed again. 'Where did that truck come from?'

My companion didn't answer. When the truck stopped alongside us, she began watching as the people crammed inside its bed jumped out the back. A bright spotlight fixed above the house's façade shone down on them. They were a mixture of men and women, young and old – or so it appeared to me from their movements and the shapes of their bodies. Exactly as had happened the first time, I couldn't make out their faces because the light falling on them was presently switched off. And the light that seeped out toward us from the windows wasn't sufficient to see them clearly. What's worse, they were all silent, only coughing gently here and there. Some seemed to be emitting groans, muffled and intermittent.

The young lady was too busy with the new arrivals to pay me any mind. It looked like she was counting them as they marched through the large iron gate, located on the other side of the house, which one of them had hurriedly opened. Then it occurred to me to jump back into the car and make my escape. And indeed, I slunk toward it like a thief, approaching the driver's side door. I squinted through the closed window to see if the key was still in the ignition. Then, all of a sudden, the young lady called out to me from afar, 'Did you forget something in the car?'

'Yes! I did!' I replied, also yelling.

With resolute determination I opened the door and reached toward the ignition. Damn! The key wasn't there.

I slammed the door angrily and returned to my place to wait until the jailer had finished her task. After they had all entered and the gate had closed behind them, she hurried back to me and took a key out of her purse. She opened the main door, stood on the threshold, and said, 'Come in.'

Chapter Two

The illuminated entrance hall was spacious and, besides a few chairs, empty. We advanced slowly toward a side door next to a long, elegant mirror cut in the shape of a tree. I saw my reflection in it. Strange, I said. Is that me? If I hadn't also caught the reflection of the young woman exactly as she appeared, I would have sworn I was the victim of an optical illusion. The mirror showed me with a thick black moustache. My sideburns and the hair on my head were tinged with white. When we passed through the door, I felt above my upper lip to make sure I had no moustache, but I couldn't ascertain whether the hair on my head had indeed been touched with age.

At the head of the room stood an opulent desk where a man with a large, bald head sat talking on the telephone while a woman next to him wrote. He may have been dictating a letter, for he was looking at the page before her as he attended to the receiver. The man wore a uniform I couldn't quite place. His copper buttons – or were they gold? – glinted whenever he moved. Both he and his female colleague were around fifty, or so I reckoned. Shortly after we entered the room, the man put the telephone receiver aside. He stood up and turned to the woman. 'Take care of the matter when I return,' he said.

I thought he was going to approach us, but he left with apparent haste from the door closest to him, shutting it behind him.

The woman raised her face toward us for the first time. 'I was afraid you would be late,' she said to my companion as she took her glasses off. 'Why don't you two sit down on that couch?'

She gestured with her glasses toward a sofa in a remote corner of the spacious room.

'Let the doctor sit down,' my lady friend replied. 'I'm a little busy.'

I had hardly sat down when she hurried out of the same door from which the man had exited. A few moments later, another young woman came through it wearing a sleeveless blue dress and holding a collection of papers she placed on the desk. Then she made a beeline for the couch. I was seated on one end of it; she sat down on the other. The woman behind the desk put her glasses back on and became engrossed in sorting through the piles of files lying before her, not even bothering to lift her eyes.

The new young lady cleared her throat softly as if to break the silence between us, or so I thought. She then edged closer to me, causing me to scrutinize her puerile face. Her hair was short, her eyes wide and brightly gleaming. She chewed on her lower lip, which glistened with a natural rouge. Her face reminded me of something I couldn't quite place, something childlike, innocent, clean, exuding the fragrance of a wild rose. 'What's your name?' I whispered to her.

She placed her index finger over her lips and pointed to the gray-haired lady sitting behind the grandiose desk. She approached me until we were touching. Then she lifted her hands, took my face in them, and pulled me toward her in a long, hot kiss. I didn't resist. She'd barely raised her lips from mine when I came back for more, closing my lips over her mouth, sucking her lips greedily, sucking the nectar from her tongue, with her fingers planted in my hair, playing with it. She suddenly withdrew from me with alarm, and both of us glanced at the woman sitting at the grandiose desk. But she was still too preoccupied with her files to pay us any mind. The young woman reclined on an arm of the couch and gestured with her hands for me to approach. So I approached, inclined above her, and devoured her lips once again. When I reached for her breasts, she helped me slip a hand under her shirt and take out from under her bra, with some difficulty, her breasts, plump and ripe, each one filling my hands with energy and vigor. I devoured them, a luscious feast my body cried out for after all my boredom, uncertainty, and worry.

She brought her mouth close to my ear, licked it, and whispered, 'Why did you resist me in the car?'

I felt as if she'd poured a bucket of cold water over me. I sat up straight, facing her, and regarded her closely. 'What!' I replied, whispering. 'Are you the same young lady?'

She let out her sweet, clear, sarcastic laugh that I couldn't mistake. 'I tricked you, didn't I?'

'But your long black hair…'

'Ah, that was a wig I took off in a matter of seconds.'

My voice was raised in spite of myself. 'Impossible! Impossible!'

'What's wrong, doctor?' the gray-haired lady suddenly said from behind her desk. 'What's impossible?'

'This sorry state I'm in, ma'am,' I replied despondently.

She directed her next question to the young lady, as if to address her in a special language I didn't understand. 'What's wrong with our friend there?'

'I think he's a bit upset,' she replied with astonishing coldness after straightening up and sitting upright. 'Also, he came without his medical bag.'

She turned to me. 'You even forgot the stethoscope, doctor!' she added. 'No problem. We have lots of medical instruments, it's not important.' Like the greatest fool in the world, she returned her own echo: 'It's not important.'

'What's important is the patient,' I added, as if to display some kind of awareness or understanding of my situation. 'Where's the patient?'

With her wide, beaming eyes, she looked into mine, which were miserable and perplexed. And with an expressionless face, she said, 'What patient? We have no patients here.'

'Then why have you brought me here?'

'Necessity knows no law, doctor.'

I watched her, her face still expressionless, as she extended her foot, encased in an elegant, black high-heeled shoe, and fondled my own foot in its thick brown leather one. Then, with the tip of her shoe, she raised the edge of my pant leg off my ankle and rubbed my shin.

I almost lost my mind! I withdrew my foot and retreated to the edge of the couch when the telephone on the desk rang with a disturbing power.

The gray-haired lady raised the receiver. 'Hello... yes,' she said. 'Yes, yes. He's here. Okay, one moment.'

She held out the receiver toward me. 'They want you on the line,' she said.

I was astonished. They wanted *me*? Who even knew I was here?

I went over to the telephone, took the receiver and said, 'Hello!'

A man's voice I didn't recognize came over the line, addressing me like an old friend. 'Hey there, doctor! How are you? Sorry to make you wait. As you know, our problems begin at nightfall. But they're strictly security matters; they don't concern you. What's important is that you've finally come.'

'Who are you anyway?' I yelled at him through the receiver. 'And what do you care about me coming or not? What is this ridiculous game?'

My telephonic interlocutor guffawed. 'Don't lose your temper, I beg you. Do you really forget that fast?'

'Forget what?'

'Our meeting on the sidewalk of the Great Square. Come on, doctor!'

'What? Are you the man... uh... the man with the long black coat?'

'The very same! I'll see you in a few minutes. I beg your pardon again for making you wait.'

He hung up.

I had hardly returned to the couch when the man with the formidable bald head and the uniform gleaming with gold buttons approached me, but with extreme respect this time. 'Is the gentleman ready?' he asked, bowing slightly. 'Everyone's waiting for you.'

I shot a questioning glance to my companion sitting silently on the other side of the couch. She gestured with her eyes and a nod of her head that I should go with the man. She even got up and approached me, encouraging me to get up. I obeyed and walked behind him as she accompanied me.

We entered a long, dark corridor that led to another corridor, lit only by a red light at the end of it. The light hung above a wide, iron double door, like backstage doors in theaters. Then I've been invited to attend a play, I said to myself. Not bad. We shall see.

One of the doors opened, and we went in. We turned once, maybe twice, before I found myself surrounded by what looked like curtains, through which my guide pushed me onto a somewhat narrow yet extremely well-lit stage. In the middle of the stage there was a table behind which three chairs stood in a row. On top of the table was a microphone. Another man—perhaps the man with the long jacket himself?—greeted me warmly and led me to the middle chair. He sat on my right, and the young lady sat on my left.

The audience chamber was somewhat wide, or so it appeared to me, for it wasn't illuminated at all. It was filled with people still clearing their throats, still fidgeting in their seats, which creaked and screeched, until I took my seat behind the speakers' table. A silence charged with an inexplicable anticipation fell in the hall. Once again, from my extremely well-lit position, I scrutinized the faces of those sitting before me. And once again, disappointment was my lot. The faces could hardly be seen, or at least I couldn't distinguish them – except for gleaming points of light that could have been the audience's eyes, or the spectacles that some of them wore. I remembered my companion's expression, 'Necessity knows no law.' What necessities had brought me here? And what would I lecture about to the folks in the audience? Why was this lecture necessary?

The master of ceremonies, who was on my right (why didn't he sit in the middle, as MCs usually do?), stood up, pulled the microphone toward himself, and, after coughing gently, raised it to his mouth. 'Ladies and gentlemen,' he said, 'it wasn't easy for us to summon our speaker here this evening because of the emergency circumstances of which you are aware. But we have, as you see, not only overcome those difficulties but also ensured your gracious presence here as well. We beg your pardon if you encountered any disturbance or distress on your way to this auditorium, which has long been graced by your presence within its walls. We do not doubt that, had you been unable to attend tonight, you would now be in your homes wondering, perhaps with a great deal of sadness and regret, what occurred here and what is to occur, what was said and what is to be said, not only in this auditorium but in the many other rooms connected to it, where you have often wandered at your leisure, conversing with one another. Our speaker, Dr. Nimr Alwan, needs no introduction.'

Nimr Alwan? Was I Nimr Alwan? I had now discovered the secret behind all their strange behavior. They had mistaken my identity, and that was that. I didn't hesitate to interrupt the MC immediately, so I pulled the microphone toward me, and in a voice not devoid of annoyance, said, 'But Mr. Speaker, I'm not Dr. Nimr Alwan.'

The MC paid no attention to my interruption, instead reclaiming the microphone and raising his voice to overcome the clamor that had begun issuing from the hall. 'As I said, our speaker Dr. Nimr Alwan needs no introduction. He can be as humble as he likes, but we're all aware of his great service to medicine in this city, just as we're all aware of his many publications that—'

'What publications?' I yelled with stubborn insistence. 'I haven't published a single book in my entire life!'

Then one of the audience members sitting in the first row stood up, saying, 'We kindly ask that the speaker not interrupt the MC, please.'

So I addressed him directly. 'If you want me to give a lecture,' I said, 'I'll give you a lecture about the following topic: I am not Dr. Nimr Alwan. I'm sure he's a fine man. But I – and I don't mean to belittle him – I don't know him! I've never even heard his name before.'

'We agree!' he replied.

He sat back down as the MC turned to me and said, 'Then the doctor should be so kind as to proceed. He'll find that we're all ears.'

I stood up, reached into my jacket's inside pocket, and took out the small notebook I always carried with me. I flipped through a few pages, giving the impression that I was reviewing my lecture notes.

'My dear ladies and gentlemen,' I said, 'I'm glad to hear that you're all ears. But what I'd like to delve into with you this evening may not require you to listen closely or to pay very much attention.'

Suddenly, the light shined down from some unknown place upon a man in the middle of the hall who stood up and mounted his chair so that everyone could see him. Gesticulating such that I feared he would fall off his chair, he cried out, 'I hereby refuse to hear this! Just as I hereby accuse Dr. Nimr Alwan of deceiving us from the first, by distracting us from the real issue that brought us together this evening.'

Then a second man, following the first's example, stood on the seat of his chair and called out, another light having fallen upon him: 'We didn't come here to listen to a lecture on medicine. We refuse to listen. And I second what my colleague Professor Mahmoud just said in accusing our speaker, Dr. Alwan.'

At that moment I recognized both men definitively! They were Mahmoud Hassan and Sami al-Imam, the famous actors. Were they speaking for themselves or, given their surfeit of excitement, were they acting? I then resolved to adapt to the new situation, so at the top of my lungs, I shouted, 'There's something fishy going on here! Can't you all smell it too?'

'Our speaker is evading, ladies and gentlemen!' yelled Mahmoud Hassan, still standing on his chair. 'This is how they shirk responsibility! They evade!'

Before I could answer, the light fell upon a young lady at the back of the hall. I saw her walk down the side aisle and approach the stage, the light accompanying her. She grasped the microphone. 'Yes, yes,' she said powerfully, 'they all evade. With the exception of our speaker this evening. Ask me! I've known him for a long time.'

She knows me?! I thought. I haven't seen her before in my life!

She continued uninterrupted. 'That he is Dr. Nimr Alwan is certain, one hundred percent. Do you remember me, doctor? Look at me closely. I'm Haifa, Haifa al-Sa'ee. You

62

deny your identity because you've forgotten it. Or, more correctly, because you deliberately and premeditatively abandoned it ever since you left me such that you've actually forgotten it. The issue, ladies and gentlemen, is not one of evasion. The issue is even greater cause for sorrow. A matter for lament. An issue of human loss and ruin it would have been worthier for Nimr Alwan to have overcome, to have defeated...'

Haifa had neared the stage, and I thought she was going to ascend it to address the audience. But she was content to turn toward the audience from her corner of the darkened hall. She held the microphone close to her lips and continued to point at me with her outstretched hand.

'This speaker of ours is a victim,' she said. 'And I'm not saying that to arouse your pity. He doesn't deserve pity. But we do have to admit that facts are facts. This victim of a man is still responsible for everything he says or does!'

I was roused to action by her words, her posture, her manner of speaking. 'What kind of lying nonsense is this?' I interrupted her angrily. 'First of all, I don't even know you, and I've never seen you before in my life. Secondly, I absolutely reject what you're claiming. I'm not the victim of anything or anybody. And I'm almost certain that you were sent to this hall as part of a scheming plot against this fine audience, which appears to have come here out of love for Nimr Alwan, or out of respect for him, even if they were also somehow coerced into coming.'

The noise level in the hall rose before I could finish talking. The MC began striking the table with his pen: 'Silence, please, silence. We'll do this by turns. You have to ask my permission to speak first anyway. Please...'

Then he surprised me by directing his words at me. 'Doctor, it appears that you're confused by all this. You came here as a speaker – that's indisputable – yet you refuse to admit that you're also here to be prosecuted...'

In one dramatic voice, the two famous actors proclaimed, 'Yes, to be prosecuted!'

The MC resumed: 'And Ms. Haifa al-Sa'ee came here to defend you. Don't you see? I encourage you to treat her as you should.'

There was nothing for me to do except sit down, exasperated, in my chair. I crossed my arms over my chest. 'Prosecute, accuse, lie, defend,' I said. 'I won't utter a single word in a situation like this.'

The hubbub returned to the hall. I noticed the two actors return to their seats, and the stage lights following them were cut off. Yet the lights continued to illuminate Haifa standing in her corner, her eyes gleaming like those of a fierce cat. The man in the first row turned toward the others, but the poor man got no stage lights to shine on him.

'I'll kindly ask you, brothers and sisters, to calm down and give your words due consideration before speaking them,' he said. 'Let's remember that Dr. Nimr Alwan came here to give a lecture, or so we led him to believe. And so, now that his world's been turned upside down, we owe him a measure of consideration, of respect.'

In the silence that followed, Haifa intoned in a voice that the microphone sent booming throughout the hall: 'The MC said I'm here for the defense. I hereby announce frankly and directly: I'm here, like all of you, to accuse. Or, let's say, I'm here for the prosecution, in the legal sense. In a little while, I'll ask the lady sitting onstage to the left of the accused to present her testimony.'

Suddenly, my companion jumped to her feet, snatched the microphone from the table, and raised it to her lips.

'What kind of testimony do you all want from me?' she asked tremulously. 'This is a farce! And I won't be a witness in a farce. I know all of you. I know each and every one of you personally. And if Ms. Haifa al-Sa'ee wants to play the role of this man's prosecutor, she's dreaming. If she wants to play the role of the district attorney, then she's *really* dreaming. And if, once upon a time, she was the lover of Nimr Alwan, then I'll kindly ask her not to air her dirty laundry in this hall. She can go looking for Nimr Alwan elsewhere. This man's name is—'

She turned to me, lowered the microphone, and leaned toward me. 'Adel al-Tibi, right?' she asked in a hushed voice. Even though I shook my head, she didn't give me the chance to state my name, for she stood up straight and raised her voice anew: 'This man's name is Dr. Adel al-Tibi!

Whoever has an accusation to level against Adel al-Tibi, let him come forward!'

A voice called out from the hall: 'Then where's Dr. Nimr Alwan?'

Haifa answered insistently from the aisle: 'He's on this stage, before your very eyes! Mahmoud Hassan, don't you recognize him?'

The light fell upon the famous actor, who didn't stand up this time but was content to remain seated. 'No, I don't recognize him,' he said. 'I haven't seen him before.'

'And you, Sami al-Imam, have you not testified against him?'

'Sorry,' the other one answered. 'I don't recognize him either.'

Haifa shrieked, her shriek so shrill that I thought she might choke. 'You're all liars, deserters, and conspirators. Every last one of you. I curse you all!'

She threw the microphone to the floor. Then the light shining on her was shut off, and she hurried back to the rear of the hall and exited through a door. She slammed the door behind her sharply. A profound silence descended upon the audience after she slammed the door, and the lights directed on the stage were immediately shut off as well. When they didn't come back on, the audience started grumbling, which gradually transformed into yelling. Someone called out, 'Come on, people, open the doors!' Another screamed, 'They're tricking us!' The commotion filled the hall as people left their seats, unable to find their way to the exits. They appeared to be falling over one another.

In the clamorous, pitch-black darkness, I felt my companion's hand slip into mine as she drew me confidently from my chair and led me aside as if she could see her way clearly through the total darkness. The MC followed me, clutching my coattails and tripping over my heels. The last thing I heard from the hall (or outside it?), once we made our way to a dimly lit corridor, was the sounds of automatic gunfire, followed once again by silence. The lights came back on.

'We didn't take that into account,' the MC said to my companion.

She confronted him harshly. 'You're still an ignorant fool,' she said.

He accepted the insult. 'I did all I could. I hoped you'd be happy with me this time,' he said miserably.

'Get out of here!' she scolded him relentlessly. 'I don't want to see your ugly face. Go back to your group in the holding pen and don't leave them until you hear from me. Understand?'

Like a banished dog with his tail between his legs, he went stumbling away. The woman stayed me with her hand in the corridor as he receded, disappearing into a door at the other end. Then she walked me silently to the door that stood opposite the first one. She took a key out of her bag and opened it. We entered a large, illuminated room where we were greeted by a woman I didn't recognize at first.

She approached me laughing and extended her hand to shake mine. 'Congratulations!' she said. 'You were wonderful!'

I was so surprised that I felt as if a rope were being wound around my neck to strangle me. It was Haifa al-Sa'ee – or the woman who just moments ago had claimed she was Haifa al-Sa'ee.

My companion embraced her, laughing. 'You were amazing,' she said, 'amazing!' She turned to me, still laughing, as if the three of us had just finished performing a rare bit of comedy. 'Nimr Alwan?' she said. 'Adel al-Tibi? Humpty Dumpty? What's your real name? Really, tell us!'

My wit couldn't match their sense of fun. They were sly and dreadful, and I had to resist them – at least until the meaning of all I'd witnessed that night was revealed.

'Tell me what your name is first?' I replied. 'You've sent my mind reeling!'

The two of them dissolved in yet more laughter before my companion came to my rescue. 'Call me whatever you like,' she said. 'Haifa, Lamia, Afra... Afra! That's a nice name. Yes, my name's Afra. And my friend and rival here, as you'll recall, is named Haifa.'

'Okay, fine,' I said angrily. 'You too, call me whatever you like. Earlier you called me Adel al-Tibi. That'll do.'

'At least temporarily,' Haifa continued. 'Even if I prefer

Nimr Alwan. Nimr, which means "tiger"... The name itself has a bite to it. I don't think the name Adel does, though...'

'Ugh!' I sighed sharply. 'Everything here has a bite to it! Who were those people you assembled in that dark hall? What was that farce?'

Afra's features (I couldn't but use that name until I discovered her real one) hardened, and her displeasure and harshness returned.

'Farce?' she replied. 'I hope the words I uttered onstage didn't deceive you. Do you want to see more of the people that, as you say, we assembled? Come, look.'

She walked toward a curtain covering the entirety of one of the room's walls, drew it back ever so slightly, and looked outside.

'Come, look,' she repeated.

I looked through the partition she'd uncovered − for the curtain covered a large window − and saw a wide-open space, more like a large courtyard in a grand old house, filled with people, some standing, some squatting, some sitting on the ground. I saw them in the light of the half-moon that had risen in the sky. The building's high walls cast dark shadows over most of them. In that moment, a new throng of people poured into them from a side gate, knocking each other about as they entered while, like as not, someone behind them drove them like cattle. Afra volunteered an explanation: 'Those who are arriving just now—they were the ones in the hall. We wanted to entertain them a bit. And educate them, too.'

'You mean torture them?'

'Torture them? A strange idea, truly!'

'And to torture me.'

'Oh, really? Have we thrown you to the lions before an audience demanding your blood?'

'Pretty much.'

Shaking her head, she turned to her colleague. 'It's no use with these people,' she said. 'They always insist on misunderstanding things.'

'Not only that,' Haifa said. 'They understand the opposite of what you mean, all down the line!'

'Do you want me to take you to the holding pen, so you can get to know your audience?' Haifa asked me with total innocence.

'My captive audience?'

'Doctor Adel, Doctor Adel, what kind of nonsense is that? Wait a bit, and you'll hear them singing the most beautiful songs. The songs may be sad – but you must know that the most beautiful songs are the sad ones. Anyway, we have things to do. We'll leave you alone here for a while. Here are some magazines. Keep yourself entertained till we return. Here's a TV and a VCR, if you'd like to use either. And here are some videotapes.'

'Thank God!' I said to myself as they were leaving. 'I'll finally get to be alone. And I'll go visit those people to learn the truth from them.'

Their footsteps grew farther and farther away until they faded away entirely. I waited two or three minutes. Then I headed for the door and opened it. I discovered that it led to a closed antechamber with two doors. When I tried one of them, I found it locked. The second door was also locked. Exasperated, I retraced my steps back into the main room and collapsed into a large leather armchair, grumbling with displeasure. I shut my eyes for a spell, hoping to open them and see that everything had changed.

Chapter Three

But no. When I opened my eyes, nothing in the room had changed. So I hurried over to the curtain and drew it back, hoping to catch the eye of someone in the square. But the curtain, once drawn, revealed a blank wall. There was no window! I almost dashed my head against the wall in desperation as I repeated, 'Impossible, impossible!' I struck the wall with my hand. It was a real wall, no doubt about that. Where was the window, then?

There was a large, identical curtain on the opposite wall. I ran over to it and yanked it aside violently. *There* was the window! I felt a powerful sense of dizziness, and had I not leaned on a nearby chair, I would have collapsed on the ground. I regained my composure, looked through the window, and said to myself, 'I should expect anything! I won't be surprised again, no matter what I see! What's important is that I find a way out of this fix.'

From the window I saw only the darkness, apart from several illuminated windows on the third or fourth floor of the large building it appeared I was in. I had surely ascended some steps I hadn't taken note of! As in the other 'window,' it occurred to me that I was looking out over a kind of city square, but a darkened one. I tried to distinguish a thing or a person in the illuminated windows but to no avail. I pricked up my ears to perhaps hear the 'audience' I'd seen a few minutes ago – singing or making a racket, it didn't matter – but it appeared that the glass, like the wall, was impenetrable, with no leaves or panes to open. I noticed that the air conditioning was on, bringing a cool, moist breeze.

I turned toward the television. With great boredom and impatience, I pressed the ON button. A crowd was clapping for a man addressing them from a stage. I turned the sound dial up to hear what he was saying. Damn! It was broken, so I was left with just a silent picture of a man talking excitedly, his hands moving ceaselessly, a crowd interrupting him with its applause. Doubtless another lecture, but one more successful than mine. I took a magazine from a low-lying table and sat down bitterly, flipping through its pages.

A short while later, the crackle of static sounded from the TV. Then the image changed, and the sound returned. A beautiful young woman—was she perhaps my jailer, my friend, Afra? She looked a lot like her, even if her hair was now long and blond. (But I had learned not to regard hair, which could be changed from one style to another in half a minute, as evidence of resemblance.) Her eyes were now fixed on the camera, or, rather, on me, for I could feel her glances penetrating me, perturbing me.

'Dear viewer,' she said. 'now you can sit comfortably in your chair and follow the scene as it unfolds on screen. You can also look from the window and follow it in real time. Alternatively, you can follow the scene both from the window and through your small screen at the same time. You'll find that the close-ups on screen will, at times, produce a pleasure not facilitated by viewing it with the naked eye.'

I got up fast and looked out the window. Suddenly, the square was arrayed like a broad stage, and I gazed at it as if I were in an uppermost loge in an opera house. The lights were set up theatrically, to include the overhead lights, the side lights, and the footlights. But the stage was totally empty.

On the TV screen, the scene was exactly the same. But I saw what resembled black ants creep onto the edge of the stage. I directed my gaze from the window downward to see a throng of people (where had they come from in such numbers – men and women of all ages?) climbing onto the stage with difficulty, pushing each other up, helping and hindering each other. The numbers of those ascending were growing fast, and no sooner had they found a place to stand onstage than they started in with violent movements, raising their hands in the air and waving them. This is how it would go: one of them would decide to stand under a blazing light and start holding forth. Then, someone else would push him aside to occupy his place and begin speaking in his turn, until the stage thronged with actors and actresses, all intoning a long, simultaneous monologue. Intoning? The truth is that they were causing a racket: shrieking, singing, moaning as if they'd lost their tongues, until they devolved into uttering nonsensical noises from their throats. I didn't know what they meant by it. Some sounds resembled the lowing of cattle, others braying, and some were exactly like howling. Yet screaming was the most prevalent. I heard it all at once, both from outside the window and from the television. When I turned the dial to lower the sound, it didn't fade away but remained loud and horrid. The close-ups that appeared on the accursed screen emphasized the gaping, twisted mouths with drool dribbling out the corners, the bulging eyes overflowing with tears, and the outstretched fingers searching above their heads for unknown objects they sought to cling to. And the screams, variegated and melding together, grew ever sharper and more chaotic.

I stopped up my ears with both hands, but the terrifying noise continued to fill my head. I cast my eyes about, searching for a rod, bar, or anything heavy to break the window with. Perhaps I could smash it above the actors' heads and put an end to this loathsome buffoonery. I could only find a straight-backed chair, which I raised with both hands and, with all the strength I could muster, sent it crashing into the window. But the chair's legs shattered and fell at my feet. The glass remained unchanged, impregnable. When I picked up a chair leg and, with all my resolution, struck the TV screen, it crumbled to pieces. The images vanished. But the sounds continued with all their strength and discord. I drew the curtains over the window and returned to the large leather armchair, surrounded by the screaming, lowing, braying, howling, just as the ocean's waves and fury surround a drowning swimmer who yet does not drown. At that moment I let out a long scream that rent my throat. I twisted in torment in my chair and heard myself utter another crazed scream, trying to stop it but unable to. During my third scream, I felt myself suffocating. I couldn't get any air. I lost consciousness for I knew not how long.

When I woke up, I could hear myself breathing loudly. I held my breath. There was a deep silence, total calm, uninterrupted save by the sound of the central air conditioning, whose duct above the door sent forth its gentle breeze.

The television had gone silent, and the sounds from outside had ceased. I stood up. With a great deal of hesitation and alarm, I approached the curtain and drew it back a bit. From the window I could only see darkness below and three or four illuminated windows in my building. I resolved to search the square for any trace of the stage and the actors, but nothing was there except for the darkness. Before I withdrew from the window – after feeling a sharp pain in my neck and throat, perhaps because of my miserable screaming – I spied someone moving below. I wasn't sure of it, so I continued to focus my gaze on the figure. From that distance, it looked to be moving along the wall.

Suddenly the figure beamed a flashlight my way. I was certain I was the target of its beam, for the light struck my window and moved right and left with my face glued to the window, in the middle of its ring of light. Yes, that person was targeting me and wanted to tell me something.

'What do you want?' I yelled at them. 'What do you want?'

No sound reached me. But they raised and lowered the light, signaling for me to descend. So, at the top of my voice, as I signaled to them by placing my hand on my chest to emphasize the meaning of my question, I asked, 'Do you want me to go down to you?'

Then I said to myself: But how could I go down, and where? The flashlight went out, leaving its blinding glare in my eyes. For a few minutes afterwards I was unable to see anything in the pitch dark outside.

I determined to leave, however much it cost me. I opened the door and went out into the antechamber. From there I headed toward the door on the right, which I'd found locked some time before. I was determined to break it if necessary. I turned the knob, and it gave way. It opened! I was overjoyed. But I was confronted with the bald man with the gold buttons speeding toward me, panting. 'Thank God!' he said. 'I've found you! I didn't know which room you were in. Though I was sure you were in one of the rooms in this wing. That's why I unlocked the doors in all the antechambers.'

I didn't quite grasp his meaning as I accompanied him to some stairs we descended. 'How did you open them all?' I asked him.

'From the control room. I can lock or unlock all the doors in the building just by pressing a button here or a button there. I was sure you'd try to leave once you found the doors unlocked. Anyway, the important thing is...'

'What's the important thing?'

'You're wanted in the Blue Room.'

'The Blue Room? Are you sure? Positive? Doubtless you also have a Red Room, and a Green one,' I added, chortling. 'But only after we've finished with the Black Room, of course.'

'Very funny, doctor,' he interrupted, his rancor obvious. 'Act your age, please.'

He began to walk faster, and I was forced to keep up. We entered another dark antechamber, which led us to more doors. He opened one of them.

'Go ahead, doctor,' he said, pushing me inside forcefully.

I'd hardly taken a step through the door when he shut it firmly behind me. I found myself in a room with walls that were actually blue, a blue ceiling, and blue curtains, all lit by a lamp on a large table and two others, each standing in a corner and casting their light on the ground. That drew my attention to the Persian rug adorning the floor, which seemed rather spacious, given the lack of furniture. In the first few moments I didn't notice the person sitting on the couch in a dark corner of the room until a strange movement emanated from them: they raised their arm high and directed a ring of bright, shining light from a flashlight at the ceiling.

'Do you recognize me?'

After a fleeting moment, I called out, 'Souad?'

She was wearing a long black dress that reached her feet. Its loose, flowing sleeves covered her wrists.

She switched off the flashlight and got up to approach me. 'What?' she asked. 'Were you scared?'

'No,' I said. 'But I was surprised.'

'Because I found out where you were?'

'Was that you waving at me with the flashlight in the square?'

'Who else would it be?'

'What's with that funereal dress?'

She laughed self-confidently, sure in the knowledge that I loved her, that I had often told her: *Nothing but an earthquake or a disaster will save me from your love.* She dropped the flashlight to the side, and I embraced her, kissing her on the lips. And then, as my mouth grazed hers, her cheeks, her temples, I was overcome by an extreme languor. I was so weary I could hardly stand. I pulled her over to the chaise longue and sat her on my lap, her arms wrapped around my neck.

'Adel, my love,' she whispered, her mouth close to my ear. 'Are you exhausted, or are you just frightened?'

'Adel? Did you say Adel?'

'Isn't that what they call you here?'

'Souad, are you on their side in this evil game, too?'

'Not at all, not at all, my love. I'm on your side, in your game, in your game alone.'

She lifted her hand until it reached the switch of the floor lamp near the couch. Then she turned it off. The other lamps were extinguished along with it. Only a faint red light remained, emanating from the same floor lamp nearby.

'It looks like you know this room well,' I said.

'I know everything,' she whispered.

She wrapped her arms around my neck once more and closed her lips over my mouth with a hunger that bewitched me. I found her forwardness strange because, from my knowledge of Souad, she always pretended to lack initiative in matters of love and resisted when confronted with my attempts, even if temporarily, in order to better inflame my passion. When my hand settled in her lap, I noticed that her dress, from the waist to the hem, had a row of large black buttons. I began undoing them one by one as she giggled in my face, saying, 'No, no...' until I undid them all.

One half of her ample dress fell to the side, dropping to the ground to reveal her exquisite thighs. I began running my hand over them, polished, throbbing, and delicious, whose touch enlivened me as though I'd downed a spirit that began working on me instantly. Then I slipped a hand between them and slid it up over her smooth, tight flesh as she coquettishly closed and unclosed her thighs, whispering: 'No, no, please...' Then she brought them together so my hand would rise to the lower part of her belly.

In that splendid, cursed moment, she closed her thighs powerfully over my fingers, shoved them away from her, and jumped off my knees to stand before me. She laughed and laughed as I sat there before her on the chair like a captive. Again she reached for the switch of the floor lamp and turned on all the lights. For a few seconds the light overwhelmed me such that I couldn't distinguish exactly what I saw.

'Was it really that easy to trick you?' she asked, resuming her derisive laugh. She raised her index finger flirtatiously to scold me as if I were a child who'd wet himself.

'How could you do that, huh?' she asked. 'And so fast! Souad! Did you immediately believe I was Souad? Didn't you ask yourself how Souad could have materialized tonight, and in this place? Aren't you ashamed of yourself? What if Souad really were here – in this room, behind the curtains, for example – and saw what you did with me?'

I got up deliberately slowly, swept away by a wave of anger that sent me hurtling toward her to tear her apart. I resisted that current, trying to understand something—anything— clear and obvious before committing my crime. She was the same woman—Afra, Lamia, I don't know who—and the lower part of her black dress still revealed most of her white legs. She didn't look a bit like Souad except in her slender, upright posture.

I approached her. I felt my hands flexing like talons I would soon close around her throat. My voice could hardly escape my clenched teeth. 'Bitch! Whore! I'll strangle you to death, you prostitute!'

'Not so fast, please,' she said, backing away from me. 'Don't get me wrong, I beg you.'

The tone of ridicule was still apparent in her voice. That only increased my wrath.

'Bitch, whore... I'll kill you, I will...'

'You can't take a joke... and you can't handle the truth... enough, enough, Nimr, Adel, Doctor X... the act is over.'

As she retreated before me, her back came up against the door. It opened for her immediately, she disappeared through it, and it closed upon me as I stood there. I tried to open it, but it wouldn't budge. I rammed it with my shoulder, but I only ended up hurting myself.

I was choked with rage, so I began kicking the door forcefully. They were torturing me. I didn't know why. What did they want from me? My knees couldn't support me anymore. I collapsed next to the door and crumpled into a heap on the Persian rug. I tried with all my might not to pass out. Finally, in a voice that roared in my throat, violent and resolute, I yelled, 'You sons of bitches! Let me out of here! Let me out!'

My face fell to the carpet, and I could feel myself inhaling the dust, my mouth hanging open. I was unable to move, and my heart beat violently against my ribcage. I stayed like that for a long time, listening with extreme attention in case I heard a sound behind the door or beneath the floor. But I could only hear my sharp panting. Moreover, it seemed not to come from me but from the hoarse throat of an animal, which only terrified me more.

Yet after a while, my panting began to subside, and my pulse slowed. A dilatory numbness flowed through my body, allowing me to move my head and stretch my legs until I found myself lying supine, totally relaxed, wishing for sleep. And perhaps I really did drift off.

I heard the lock turning in the door. I sensed the presence of someone behind it, pushing it with what seemed like trepidation. But the door bumped into me because I was lying in front of it. Still on the ground, I edged away from it until it opened.

'Ah! You're here! On the floor? Doctor, why are you sleeping on the floor? Sorry we were late. Sorry...'

The Man with the Golden Buttons leaned over me and offered me his hand to help me up.

'Leave me alone. Leave me be,' I told him with a weak voice I could hardly hear myself.

'Come on, let's go, get up.'

'Leave me alone.'

'Don't be unreasonable. Give me your hand, doctor. Maybe you fell. Were you hurt?'

He stood me up and began carefully brushing the dirt off the breast and shoulders of my jacket. I noticed another man standing in the doorway watching us.

Mr. Buttons turned toward him and told him with a surfeit of respect: 'There you are, sir. It appears Dr. Nimr fell for some reason. Perhaps he fainted.'

When the man entered, I realized he was the MC whom my "lady friend" had insulted after the farce that was "the lecture" and driven off. Now he was a different man altogether: clearly confident, grim, and trying to communicate that he was far more important than I could imagine. Without so much as a glance in my direction, he headed for the desk and sat behind it like one long accustomed to presiding over sessions, meetings, and discussions. With his index finger he pointed to my friend.

'Turn on the lights,' he said. Then he opened a drawer in the desk and took out a stack of papers. He drew the table lamp toward them so that more light could shine on them. Meanwhile, my friend Mr. Buttons obeyed his command, pressed a switch in the wall, and drowned the hall in a powerful light.

'Please, sit here,' he told me.

He led me to a straight-backed chair near the table, which I sat in while looking at the MC. For the first time, it occurred to me that I knew him, that I'd known him for a long time. Or was I delusional because of my destabilizing condition? Wasn't it him – goddammit! I couldn't remember his name. He finally looked at me, gazing into my eyes.

'Aren't you—' I said. 'Oh, I know you...'

'We met in the Great Square.'

'But your name—'

'That's immaterial, Dr. Nimr. What is important—'

'No,' I interrupted, 'it's very important for me to be sure of your identity.'

He shook his head, his lips twisted in a derisive smile. 'My identity? We're busy enough with you, and you want to flip the script?'

'Busy with me? Just as your highly respectable lady friend was a while ago?'

He looked angry. 'Quiet!' he yelled furiously. 'You're raving mad!'

'Didn't you see her when she was leaving, fleeing, from this room? And you, Mr. Buttons, didn't you see her on your way here?'

Mr. Buttons still stood to my right. 'He's dreaming, sir,' he said, addressing the MC. 'There wasn't anyone in this hall besides him before we got here.'

'I know,' he replied. 'His problem is that he has a fertile imagination, and he's quick to dream things up. Listen, doctor. I'll put you at ease. I'm Azzam Spinks. Have you heard that name before?'

'Azzam Sphinx?' I said. 'No, I don't think so.'

'Spinks, with just a *p*. Are you content now?' Then he tapped his fingers on the papers before him. 'Well then,' he added, 'we're finished with the first matter of business. Now on to the second one.'

It goes without saying that I was exhausted, pained, and full of disgust. I didn't care who that false man was. I was certain he was putting on an act that bore no relation to his actual character; that he had perhaps been forced to adopt the role of a man he himself didn't understand or care to understand; and that, after that insult from a beautiful young woman – and a deceitful one at that – who wouldn't hesitate to slap a dignified man like him if necessary, he was no longer capable of affecting me or regaining my respect for his spent pride. Anyway, as I was saying, in such a situation, I didn't care much about a man enumerating a second point and a third and a fourth, as if he were the Master of Reason and Logic in that room, which was blue for no particular reason. Let him say what he would — that's what I told myself. Whether his name was Spinks or Sphinx or Shithead, I wouldn't discuss anything with him until a door opened from which I could exit of my own free will.

Perhaps he could sense the thoughts that beset me. He narrowed his eyes, focusing them on my face, then relaxed his face suddenly. He took a cigar out of a sumptuous case before him and offered it to me. I put it between my lips, and he handed me a lighter, which I lit the cigar with. I gave him back the lighter, which he put in his breast pocket. Attempting a kind of artificial good cheer, he addressed the man standing behind me.

'Bring us some coffee, Alewi.'

Alewi had hardly left when the man showered me with his artificial cheeriness for a few seconds. I exhaled the smoke of the Cuban cigar and prepared myself for an inescapable period of absentmindedness.

'The second point,' he said, 'isn't the most important thing I have to tell you, but we must adhere to a sequence that properly clarifies matters and, speaking of points, dots the i's and crosses the t's, as they say. What I care about is that you don't equivocate with me. Because if you do, how am I going to be clear and understandable in front of the others? You can't make someone understand a particular issue that you yourself don't understand in the first place. Otherwise, you're like someone spouting riddles, not from wisdom but because he wants to fool one into believing that his thoughts are profound, difficult to explain and communicate. Are you with me? Let's say you were asked to write a book, for example, or, say, a lengthy study, about a topic that's foreign to you. What would you do? You'd review the sources. Very well. If you found the sources to be few and rare, you'd adhere to those few, rare sources and extract something worthy, even with your lack of sources. But if you found that none of the books you consulted discuss that topic – I mean, if you found that none of your sources and none of anyone else's helped you in your study, what would you do? One of two things: either you'd bow out and not write anything at all. Or, or – pay attention, please, to what I'm saying – you'd use your own repertoire to make things up. You might claim you extracted some of your material from sources—imaginary ones, of course. Or you could merely contrive and fabricate, and all the so-called sources can go to hell. That situation is what we face in most of our daily activity. Contrivance, fabrication, or, if you want to use a nicer word, innovation. Are you still with me?'

He stopped to wait for my reaction.

'Yes?' I said.

'Are you still with me?'

'Yes, yes. Please continue.'

I took a drag on the cigar and then nonchalantly tapped the ashes onto the Persian rug. He lifted the stack of papers in his hands so I could take a good look at it.

'These papers are an example of what I'm talking about,' he said. 'No, I won't trouble you with reading them out loud, and I won't burden you by giving them to you to read afterwards. They're here as evidence, as a document. Documentation is an art whose importance in our social, political and intellectual life we've only recently begun to grasp. History accumulates in these words and papers, and we must learn how to make so much spilled ink beneficial to our age and the ages to come. Pardon! I mean this metaphorically. These papers, as you can see – well, most of them – were printed on a copy machine. And innovation – no, creativity – is fundamental to them. Here we practically imitate the Creator, the Almighty, in that, every now and then, we create things from nothing. Ah, the coffee's arrived!'

I didn't understand a word of what he was saying. For most of the time, and from my uncomfortable position in the straight-backed chair, I was watching his lips move instead of his eyes. Are those lustrous teeth of his real? I asked myself. No way. They gleamed like pearls – artificial, no doubt. Ah, the coffee! And a glass of water along with it. Alewi, the former Mr. Gold Buttons, served us from a silver tray that shined like his large bald pate. I put the coffee cup on the table and downed the glass of water in one gulp while Alewi served Mr. Spinks the other cup of coffee. Then he whispered something in his ear. Spinks didn't reply at first, and he appeared hesitant to respond. 'I have no objection,' he said softly.

Alewi came back over to me, took a thick envelope out of his inside jacket pocket, handed it to me, and left. I'd taken a few sips of coffee, which, after the cold water I'd tossed down, was as delightful as the rivers of paradise. I looked at the envelope and took another sip.

Spinks began talking again as he held the coffee cup, sipping from it now and then, granting me no respite until I opened the envelope to read what was inside. I put it on the desk in front of me. I saw that the back of the envelope read:

Dr. Adel al-Tibi

The two words 'Nimr Alwan' had been erased yet were still legible despite the erasure. They were followed by the words 'Adel al-Tibi' as a subsequent correction.

Spinks continued to expatiate:

'And of course, we're sometimes surprised by what we don't regard. The thing we spend days preparing for could be tossed about by a storm from we know not where, throwing all our plans to the winds in a single moment, just as storms send leaves flying. But even these surprise storms themselves could be part of the operational plan in place or, if you will, part of the game. And by the word 'game,' I don't mean that here we spend our time entertaining ourselves. The game here is dangerous: more like a game of chess, which requires a mix of intelligence and cunning, a mix of adventure and deception, a game in which, if you lose, you could also lose your head. Oh yes. These words of mine, this time, are no metaphor. Rather, I hope that later you'll have a few minutes to ask Alewi to show you the Room of Honor so you can see how we've recorded in beautiful diwani calligraphy the names of those who've played this game and lost. It's a beautiful room, what with its wondrous calligraphy recording some shining examples of governance with which our heritage abounds and which we would do well to keep alive in the minds of the people as a reminder and a lesson. Lately we've engaged the services of three well-known artists to paint the portraits of those good-hearted 'Losers' in concordant oil paintings. We'll hang them in chronological order. They're transposing them and enlarging them from regular photographs, but they're making them into artistic marvels, each one of which the viewer will delight in contemplating, drawing inspiration from the looks and features of all those who ventured and lost—their heads! But they didn't lose eternal renown, at least for those wishing to recall their memory—the memory of their risks and hazards, their errors, their ends...'

It seemed to me that Azzam Spinks was not going to cease expatiating and that he took pleasure in showering me with his thoughts, unaware that I paid him no attention. I could hardly follow anything he said. I was forced to interrupt him.

'Pardon me, Mr. Azzam. That letter I just received—don't you think it's best I open it, to learn what's inside?'

He wasn't pleased that I'd dragged him down from the heights of his eloquence to the mire of the present moment, which threatened to scatter his thoughts entirely. 'The letter?' he said astonished. 'Ah, the letter!' Then he scowled. 'Alewi told me it was urgent,' he added. 'Sorry, doctor, I got carried away talking. Go ahead, open it.'

I crushed out the cigar on the table and picked up the letter. I'd barely broken the seal when all the lights went out − even the soft red light that had aided me in my failed romantic adventure with Afra. I yelled, for I suspected it was prearranged and intentional.

'Sir, you have turned out the lights. Because you don't want me to read this letter.'

'Not at all, not at all,' he replied. 'Maybe the electricity went out for some reason, but that rarely happens. On top of that, we have generators for these contingencies.'

'Where's your lighter? Light it so we can see our way.'

'My lighter? I'm not carrying a lighter.'

'Amazing! Didn't you just give me your lighter a few minutes ago for me to light my cigar?'

'Not at all. I imagine it's you who has a lighter − or maybe a box of matches?'

'I'm not carrying a lighter or a box of matches,' I said, annoyed. 'This game of yours is up, and it's totally unnecessary.'

I got up from my chair, trying to remember the location of the curtain so I could open it, when I remembered that it was right behind him.

'The curtain's behind me,' he said as if he'd read my mind. 'But it doesn't cover a window. Just like in most of these rooms. Here!'

I heard him push his chair aside and draw back the curtain in vain. I remembered that my lady friend had surprised me in the room with a flashlight, and I didn't recall her picking it up off the couch when she fled. In the darkness I retreated cautiously to where I remembered the couch being. It was, by my estimation, about five or six meters behind me. I found it. I passed both my hands over the soft cushions in search of the flashlight. Then I got down on my knees and began looking for it by groping about the floor alongside the couch, hoping it had fallen to the ground from the young lady's sudden movement when jumping off my lap. But my hands fell on the shoes of a person standing above me.

'Ah! Did you find the flashlight?' I asked.

'Which flashlight, doctor? Get a hold of yourself. I'll try to find the door and open it so we can go out together.'

I sat down on the couch.

'Even if you find the door,' I said, 'you'll find it locked. Do you have a key? Of course not. And it's locked electronically too, most likely.'

Spinks didn't respond. I heard him moving. It appeared he'd found the door, and he began pulling on the knob, which rattled but didn't open. 'Damn you and whoever locked you too!' he grumbled. Then he began pounding the door with his fists.

'Take it easy, take it easy,' I told him. 'Get a hold of yourself, sir, just as you advised me to do. Why make all that racket? Why don't you come sit on this nice, soft cushion until the Good Lord sets things straight? Come here and tell me the story of your life.'

'My life?' he said in a voice impetuous and rash. 'Pure hell, from beginning to end. Do you know what I mean, doctor? The cheapest thing in life is death. As for me, that son of a bitch is lording it over me. I don't doubt for a second that this is a scheme of that lowlife Alewi.'

This time it was my rightful turn to laugh. 'Alewi? The poor man with the buttons?'

'Don't let his wretchedness fool you. He's a snake in the grass. He's after my job, the little bastard. He'd murder his own father to get it. He pimps himself out to everyone in the organization—men and women, it makes no difference. Beware of him. Treat him as he deserves. Spit in his face, then throw him a few pennies to insult him twice over. Ugh, it's no use with this door. Where are you?'

'Here, here,' I said.

He stumbled about until he fell into my lap. I pushed him aside, and he got settled near me on the couch, panting and grumbling. Even though he was right up against me, I felt there was a great distance between us, a distance I didn't want to shorten. I was afraid he would touch me. A kind of calm returned to me. I wished it would endure, and I hoped it would help me regain the power to endure my situation without losing the ability to reason. 'The guard and the prisoner,' I grumbled sarcastically. Then I raised my voice:

'Who was it who said: 'Misery acquaints a man with strange bedfellows'?'

He didn't respond. After a while his panting lessened, then ceased. I thanked God for his silence, and I too kept quiet. Does he have a death wish? I asked myself. What if he died right now, in this pitch dark, right next to me? After a while, during which he made no movement whatsoever, I touched his arm with one of my fingertips. He was still there, in a profound calm. He had spoken his piece and now come to an end. End?! Terror gripped me. Had he died of a heart attack? 'Spinks, Spinks!' I yelled, punching him in the arm. A great snore like the bellow of an ox escaped his nostrils, which reassured me that at least he hadn't breathed his last.

Chapter Four

After a long time spent yearning for sleep, but to no avail, the lights came back on in the room. Or, I should say, in the hall. For, after being blinded for a few moments from the intensity of the light, a hall appeared, spacious, rectangular, and dazzling, as befits a Blue Room—all of it blue, from the ceiling to the walls, to the curtains and the furniture. Spinks lay in a profound slumber, his head drooping onto his chest. He leaned to one side on the cushion, and his light snoring was consistent with his breathing. I shook him by the shoulder, but, in his slumber, his trunk only fell along the length of the couch, and the rhythm of his snoring immediately changed. I went over to the table where the envelope lay. I still wanted to read its contents. I pulled out a paper, folded several times, and opened it. And there it was—two pages of foolscap filled with writing. I was anxious to read it before being overtaken by another 'storm' Spinks had mentioned.

I read the following:

To the Esteemed Dr. Nimr Alwan,

We, the signatories below, would like to inform you that we await you with impatience. Do not believe everything you hear or see in the Blue Room. Come quickly. Hurry!

After that, the long, wide page was crammed with a mass of signatures, not one of which I was able to read. Uninterrupted signatures, signatures running into and over each other, signed with various pens, some blue, some black, some red, which reminded me of the 'petitions' that village headmen and mayors used to present to government officials in days long past to prove that hundreds of men and their families supported them in their 'just' demands. Doubtless another scheme of Alewi's! He was playing a practical joke, the slippery old snake, that snake in the grass. If he returns, I'll ask him: What's the meaning of this huge piece of paper? What am I to do with it? Where should I go to meet those who *await me with impatience*? What a bad joke!

To express my contempt for such jesting, I tore up the letter and piled its shreds on the table.

I looked over at Spinks snoring away, immersed in sleep. How lucky he is! I thought, realizing I wouldn't be able to gain anything by him. It occurred to me to try opening the door again, but I didn't even glance at it. Fine, I thought, I'll try opening the curtains, as I did in the previous room. But my eyes fell on the stack of papers Spinks had illuminated with the table lamp. I reached for them to read, for they surely contained written reports on me.

The papers were glossy, and most of them contained elegant text printed with a typewriter, just as he'd said. They looked to be mostly photocopies. But they weren't in Arabic or English. Or French. I didn't know what language they were in. They weren't in Russian or any of the Slavic languages, for I could recognize the Cyrillic alphabet. They were in Latin letters, yet I didn't understand a single word. I flipped through them rapidly. They were all in that strange language – or that contrived language, perhaps? That 'invented' language? I threw them on the floor, headed for the curtains, and drew them violently to the left, as far as they would go. Just as I'd suspected. At the far end, the curtains revealed a door painted blue. Its knob, despite its azure, stood out. Poor Spinks! Was he too perhaps a stranger in this organization, and ignorant of its mysteries? I'd hardly placed my hand on the doorknob and begun turning it when it opened.

I entered another room that closely resembled a waiting room in a doctor's office. Along the four bright white walls stretched benches arranged for visitors to sit on. Yet no visitors sat there. On the walls hung color photos of rosy-cheeked mothers nursing their children and plump Siamese cats, purple ribbons adorning their necks. My impression that it was a patients' waiting room was confirmed. Was the Blue Room the consultation room? Or did the door in the opposite wall lead to it? I headed straight for it and opened it.

Another room, also white-walled, yet free of furniture except for a single chair where a handsome young man sat wearing a white coat. He was reading a book. Perhaps he was the doctor? Or the nurse?

He lifted his gaze toward me. He looked astonished to see me. But he remained seated.

'Would you like to see the doctor?' he asked.

'Which doctor?' I replied.

He registered astonishment once again. 'How did you get here, then, if you didn't know which doctor you wanted to see?'

Let's try my luck with him, I told myself.

'Dr. Nimr Alwan. Is he available?' I asked.

He snapped the book shut with both hands.

'Dr. Nimr Alwan is very much available,' he replied, smiling. 'He's standing right in front of me. I saw you on TV two hours ago, doctor. Are you testing me?'

'Not at all, not at all. And you, are you a doctor, or...?'

'Indeed. But I was forbidden from practicing medicine a few months ago. Do you see this white coat? I still insist on wearing it, to always remember my duty toward tormented humanity.'

He got up from his chair and approached me.

'Please, sit down,' he added.

I thanked him. 'No, please,' I said, 'return to your seat.'

'I'm tired of sitting. And tired of waiting. Do you know who occupies the room behind that door?'

'Tormented humanity?' I replied, charging my voice with the greatest possible amount of seriousness.

'Not in that room,' he said, confronting me with corresponding seriousness. 'And not on this floor. It seems to me you've lost your way.'

'A bit.'

'Strange, since there are signs on most of the doors.'

'Signs? I haven't seen a single one to guide me where I want to go.'

'This is the age of technology. Even directions are programmed in symbols and codes. And you have to know those symbols in advance, reflect on them, and follow the green, red and yellow lights and arrows that accompany them. Then you'll get to where you want to go.'

'What if you don't know all the symbols in advance, or where you want to go?'

'Ha, ha! In that case, God help you. But what's there to worry about, doctor? Sooner or later, you'll get to where you want to go. For without being aware of it, you seek a particular location your consciousness is afraid to define for you. In other words, with the ignorance you claim to possess, you're evading. It's a licit evasion because it represents salvation from pains you can do without. Before tonight, I'd never heard your name or seen you. Despite that, I've begun learning quite a bit about you.'

'Amazing. You're sharper than I am.'

'Not at all. Do you see this book?'

He lifted it for me to read its title: *The Known and the Unknown.*

'I haven't seen it before,' I said.

'It has a long chapter on you.'

'You mean it has a long chapter on Nimr Alwan.'

'Yes. And I was engrossed in it when you came in. What a weird coincidence!'

'What if I told you I wasn't Nimr Alwan?'

'Not important!'

'You don't say!'

'What's important is that I, Dr. Rassem Ezzat, am convinced that you are Nimr Alwan. And if you're not him, then you wouldn't be standing here with me now in this room. On top of that, I don't know why you're denying it, doctor. Look at this picture.' He opened the book and flipped through it until he came across a photo and raised it before me so I could see it clearly. 'Read the caption below it: Dr. Nimr Alwan.'

I snatched the book from him and scrutinized the photo. It was indeed my picture!

'Fabrication!' I yelled. 'Criminal fabrication!'

'For the most part, the author praises you. So why would he fabricate anything?'

He took the book back from me.

'I know you claim your name is Adel al-Tibi,' he added. 'And perhaps you have a design in that. That's your business, and I won't interfere in your private affairs.'

'What if I told you my name wasn't Adel al-Tibi?'

'Then you'd be telling the truth. Because you're Nimr Alwan.'

'Or Nimr Alwan either?'

'As you wish. That won't affect my personal conviction.'

'Did you know... Dr... Uh...'

'Rassem Ezzat.'

'Did you know, Dr. Rassem, that I don't care about your personal conviction?'

'Touché. Which reminds me of a saying of yours: 'Our true opinions spring from within and flow back in again.''

'Did I say that?'

'Don't be humble with me, sir. I read the transcript of the discussion between you and your students when you said, from what I remember, 'Man is not an island, sufficient unto himself, true! But what narrow isthmus links him with others, and through what raging sea does that isthmus lie?''

I laughed aloud despite the seriousness my friend had imposed on himself.

'Forsooth!' I said. '*Through what raging sea does that isthmus lie*? And how do we cross it? And the others, do they cross it in our direction? Do they not collapse into the waves that inundate it and so drown? Do we hear their voices from the other side?'

'But you affirm that we not only hear their voices but also see them waving at us wherever we turn, even though the storm could swallow their screams. It's your final refusal of the inevitability of tragedy.'

'Despite all the world's calamities?'

'That's what you yourself say. And there's a lot of evidence of that in your life and writings.'

I didn't recall ever having said such a thing. And I didn't know what he meant by *my writings*. What writings could they be, seeing as I'd never published an article, not to mention a book? For a moment or two I reconsidered and wondered whether I actually had published something once – a book or a monograph, perhaps more than one – and just forgotten. Yet I rejected that passing thought, dismissing it from my mind.

'Do you mean,' I said, 'if you screamed now, in this very room, there'd be someone there to hear you?'

'Without a doubt,' he replied without hesitation. 'But...'

'But what?'

'But that doesn't necessarily mean that whoever hears you will come running.'

'Why not?'

'Because maybe he's trapped in his own room, or maybe he's locked in.'

'Then what use is your screaming?'

'Permit me, doctor, to respond in your very own words: *To remind him of my presence here.*'

'And if he did come running to you?'

'He'd see my situation and understand.'

'And if he didn't understand your situation as you wanted him to?'

'I'd try to make him understand, to convince him. But here too, doctor, I might resort to what you yourself said.'

'Meaning?'

'I would attempt to establish the complex relationship between the I and the Thou.'

'In all truth, I don't understand.'

'Maybe you've forgotten, but I clearly recall your quoting a poet of the last century:

'You can't prove that I, speaking to you, am not you
   speaking to yourself.
'For nothing provable but irrefutable merits the proving...'

'Now you're confusing me,' I interrupted him.

'In other words,' he continued, ignoring my interruption, 'when establishing the relationship, I need to remember many things at the same time. First, that I, speaking to you, could be you speaking to yourself — as in our discussion right now — and there's quite a deep meaning in that; we could talk about it for hours. Second, the relationship is always complex. It's either a relationship between I and Thou, I and I, or Thou and Thou — and the nearly insoluble complexity that that entails. Third, after all that, the most important thing in life — the most important thing that enriches and advances it, elevates and debases it — transcends reason and affirms its turbulent effect on what lies out of the range of proof and refutation...'

I went dizzy. I no longer understood anything.

'You remember all that about me?' I asked.

'To some extent,' he said. 'In short.'

'And if I wanted to leave here, without resorting to screaming?'

'For you, nothing would be easier.'

'Then – God keep you – if you get me out of here, I'll be obliged to you and your generosity forever.'

'That's the least I could do. Come with me, please.'

He headed toward a side door painted white, which I hadn't noticed. Together we went out into a corridor, wide and well-lit. He guided me to an ascending staircase.

'All you have to do,' he said, 'is go up that staircase to the upper floor, then turn left. After a short distance, you'll find a staircase that goes down. Take it—it's the shortest way out.'

I wasn't totally reassured by his directions.

'Won't you escort me there, Dr. Jassem?' I asked.

'Rassem. Rassem Ezzat.'

'Pardon! My memory's like a sieve. Won't you escort me to the upper floor?'

'You won't need me, doctor. Anyway, I can't stray far from my post here because the other door could open at any moment. And I need to be there when it opens.'

I resigned myself to God's will.

'Thank you,' I said. 'Go back to your book.'

He extended his hand to shake mine.

'I advise you to get a copy. Remember its title: *The Known and the Unknown*.'

'Yes, yes.'

'If you run into Alewi on your way, ask him to give you a copy. You need to read what they write about you, however imprecise it is, or full of errors.'

'Of course, of course,' I said. I went up the stairs as I thought to myself: Shall I really read what they write about me? Have I gone crazy?

Chapter Five

I reached the upper corridor, which was poorly lit, and quickly turned left. A hand shot out from a black cloak to stop me. It was a pretty hand, with tapered fingers, red fingernails, many rings, and numerous gold bracelets shining around the wrist. When I discovered that the hand had become three, I thought I was the victim of an optical illusion. But no. There they were: three seated women, each one wrapped in a black cloak that covered her head and part of her face and flowed down over the rest of her body until it reached the floor so that only the tips of her feet showed. They sat bunched together on a raised seat. The three resembled statues of ebony, except that their white faces were somewhat exposed and their thickly kohled eyes were fully open as if made of crystal. Each one raised her right hand to me, then lowered it into her lap. I stopped in front of them. Were they the Fates I'd read about in myths when I was young? Did they want something from me? Did they know I was coming? But all three of them, as I stood there wondering, closed their eyes and immediately forgot me. It appeared that the middle one, after I hadn't moved a muscle while standing before them, could sense that I wanted to address them. She opened her eyes. I noticed her long, coal-black tresses that flowed down the sides of her cheeks and showed through the cloak's opening above her chest, where they rested on her ample breasts. She raised her right hand again and drew her index finger to her lips. Then she extended her bare arm through the black folds of her cloak and pointed with her finger into the depths of the corridor, whispering, 'There...'

For a second, I saw in her countenance all the contradictions of this world. I saw lamentation and promiscuity. I saw lust and self-denial. I saw temptation and restraint. I saw omnipotence and total powerlessness. I refrained from speaking before those statues burdened with their secrets and withdrew from them before the riddle could tumble down from its wondrous summit. As soon as I turned my face away, I glimpsed the top of the staircase at the end of the passage. Thank God! I hastened to it.

I had only gone down a few steps – which weren't lighted, and which the corridor's lights illuminated only faintly – when the staircase turned, and I almost stepped on the back of a man sitting on the stairs. Next to him sat another man, and on the following steps sat men and women for the extent of the staircase as it descended. On every step sat a dense line of people. I stopped for a moment to take in the situation. This time the staircase descended a great distance until it disappeared into the darkness, as into the bottom of an abysmally deep well. It was crammed full of people leaning on each other. Despite the growing darkness, I could see they were all exhausted, spent, and silent, except for the occasional cough or clearing of the throat. They had been in that state for a long time, without a doubt. I could tell I would only be able to descend by stepping between them with great difficulty. I might have stepped on their hands and legs if I did that.

The man my foot had struck stirred. He moved a bit then raised his head toward me, as if wondering what I wanted.

'Pardon me,' I said. 'I want to go down.'

'Is that so?' he answered mockingly. 'I do too.'

'You mean to say that the way is blocked?'

'As you can see.'

'What's to be done?'

'Sit on your step and wait.'

'Until when?'

'Until you're released. Have you been sentenced?'

'Sentenced? God forbid!'

'Then I'd advise you to return to wherever you came from. These stairs are for the convicted.'

In other circumstances I might have asked and probed. But in that situation, I felt only the need to find a way out to some sort of open space, and to let whatever may happen unfold. The awful feeling of suffocation returned to me, and the air was rank with human breath. But my sense of humanity overcame me.

'I'll sit with you,' I said.

This time the other man raised his head toward me.

'What for?' he asked

'In solidarity with you.'

He returned to his position and shrugged.

'As you wish,' I could hear him mutter.

His neighbor turned to him. 'Bestowing their favors upon us, I see,' he said softly.

The other man shook his head, sunk between his desperate shoulders, and sighed. 'Ahh, ahh...'

It didn't occur to me that Alewi would be lying in wait for me even there. I felt a hand pat me on the shoulder, and when I turned around, I saw the bald pate itself leaning over me. Alewi stood behind me on the step above, and, like the woman in the black cloak, he placed his index finger over his lips, ordering me to silence.

'Follow me,' he whispered.

I hesitated and remained where I was.

'The matter concerns you,' he whispered again. 'Concerns *you.*'

'You people have nothing that concerns me,' I said. I sat stubbornly on my step.

He came down next to me and leaned over me again.

'Your place is not here,' he whispered.

'And why not?' I said, almost yelling. 'All those people there, are they not human beings, just like me?'

Several heads of those seated on the nearest steps turned in my direction.

'Hush up!' a few of them said.

Alewi returned the echo, his lips close on my ear. 'Hush, doctor. I'll explain the situation to you later. Come on.'

He stood up, pulling me up powerfully by the arm. I stood up in spite of myself, ascended the stairs, and followed him. He began to hurry, his arm wrapped around mine as if I were his best friend in the whole world. We went down some stairs, we went up some stairs, and we passed through a hall or two. Alewi was silent all the while, headed toward his destination with an amazing confidence. Now and then he glanced at his watch as if he feared he'd be late for a well-established appointment.

I grabbed his arm and stopped him.

'Look, Alewi,' I said.

'Yes?'

'What's the story behind that letter you gave me in the Blue Room?'

'What about it?'

'Who sent it?'

'Did you read it?'

'Of course.'

'So I was informed.'

'But who sent it?'

Then, with a measure of boredom, as if he'd been forced to explain an issue he'd explained a thousand times before, he said, 'Doctor, I don't care who sends what to whom. Letters come in to my office, and I deliver them. As for their contents, their senders, their recipients—that's none of my business. But let me ask, if you'll permit me: Why don't you view the matter from a purely psychological perspective?'

'I don't see any psychological perspective to this matter!'

He slowed down.

'I'm embarrassed to explain something to Dr. Nimr Alwan, seeing as he's the most qualified person to elaborate on it,' he said without meeting my eye.

Before I could object or urge him to explain, he continued:

'In the depths of every human soul, there's a longing to receive messages, hidden voices, or thoughts from unknown regions that point to the existence of powers, operations, or beings that lie outside our direct consciousness and seek to make contact with the human soul. For example, wouldn't you like to receive a letter from an unknown admirer—one whom you might refuse to admit into your home if he showed up on your doorstep, while you nevertheless welcome his written words, for words are nothing but potential energy, unembodied, that carry meanings unrestricted by material boundaries? Why don't you let that obscure longing in the depths of your own soul move along of its own accord, without interference or supervision from you, without insisting on knowing the cause and the effect? Why don't you allow yourself to receive what the senses don't comprehend so you can discover what lies beyond them? Forgive me, doctor. These issues are outside my bailiwick.'

He had proved to me just how cunning he was, more so than he had before.

'Alewi!' I cried. 'How unlike Spinks you are!'

He looked at me and, for the first time, flashed a strange, devilish smile, as if he were a magician who had succeeded in pulling ten live rabbits out of his hat.

'Me?' he said. 'I am but a drop in his wide ocean, my good sir. Come on. Hurry. We're late.'

He went silent again and led me to an exquisite elevator door. He pushed the button, and it opened immediately as if it had been standing there waiting for us. Inside the elevator was a large mirror. I saw my reflection for the second time that night despite Alewi's attempt to stand between me and the mirror. Yet I pushed him out of my way so I could scrutinize my face. I was alarmed. That wasn't the face I knew myself to have! It was as if I were another man I'd never seen before in my life.

'Is this another one of your schemes, Alewi?' I yelled.

He didn't respond. In all my consternation, I didn't know whether the elevator had taken us up or down once the door opened and Alewi pulled me by the hand into a large passage where the doors followed each other in an orderly fashion, as in a hotel. The one key difference was that the doors weren't numbered. He stopped before one of them, a small sign reading "Exit" affixed to it.

'Thank God!' I said.

He pushed the door open. We entered a room. The rear part of it was divided from the front part by a barrier whose lower half was of wood and whose upper half was of glass. Over the wooden half was a counter with papers and forms arranged atop it. Behind the glass sat two young women, each with a typewriter in front of her.

Alewi took a form and thrust it toward me.

'Do you have a pen?' he asked. 'Fill it out, pronto. Please.' I took the form, spread it out on the counter, took out my pen, and read:

Your father's quadripartite name and his occupation:
Your mother's quadripartite name and her occupation:
The names and occupations of four of your paternal uncles:
The names and occupations of four of your maternal uncles:
Signature:

I paused, the pen between my fingers. I may remember the name of my father and my grandfather, but the name of my great-grandfather, and my great-great-grandfather...

Alewi noticed my hesitation, so he snatched the paper from me and took a pen out of the breast pocket of his coat with the gleaming gold buttons.

'I'll fill it out for you,' he said.

In the blink of an eye, he filled out the first line, then the second, then the third, then the fourth. He thrust the form toward me and ordered: 'Sign!'

When I hesitated again before signing, he once more snatched the paper back and inscribed what resembled a signature at the bottom. He pushed it under the glass barrier toward one of the two young ladies.

'Stamp it, please,' he said, 'and pardon us for being in such a hurry.' Wordlessly, the young woman selected a stamp from one of the many arrayed before her and stamped the form. Then she fed it into the copy machine on her right, which produced a copy in a few seconds, then another. She handed them both to Alewi, and she retained the original. She flashed me a quasi-conspiratorial smile, as if to say: *I know you didn't fill the form out yourself.* She lifted her hand ever so slightly to wave a friendly goodbye.

Once we left and the door closed behind us, Alewi handed me one of the copies of the form.

'Here, doctor,' he said. 'You might need it.'

I looked resentfully into his eyes.

'What do I have to do with it?' I asked. 'Did I fill it out?'

'What's the difference? Here, read it.'

'I refuse to read your fabrications.'

'Okay. Don't read it. But at least hold on to the copy. You might need it when I'm no longer with you.'

He folded it and planted it firmly in my side pocket. He held the other copy in his hand. Then he looked at his watch again.

'For God's sake, hurry,' he added. 'We're very late. That idiot nurse Rassem Ezzat—I clearly ordered him to take you to the Banquet Hall, but he was determined to mislead you. He always does that.'

'So now we're hurrying off to the Banquet Hall?'

'A group of politicians and intellectuals are giving a dinner party in your honor. Hasn't anyone told you?'

'Alewi, you are full of surprises!'

'But we have to go to the Archive first. It's on our way. We'll only be there a few minutes. Do you have any objection?'

'The Archive? Ah, of course. Documentation is important.'

'Yes, it is. Through here.'

He led me to a narrow elevator for which he had a special key. It took us down to an elongated, well-lit vault where lead-colored iron file cabinets, tall enough to reach the ceiling, were arranged successively down the walls in two lines that met at the far, rounded end of the vault. Some of the file cabinets had doors, and others had drawers with handles. They were all of superior quality and made of noncorrosive steel. Alewi guided me onto what resembled a metal walkway stretching down both sides of the room alongside the file cabinets. With a movement of his foot, the walkway began to move, taking us down the length of the file cabinets. We continued advancing until we reached the far end of the vault, where the two sides met and rounded off. There Alewi stopped the moving walkway.

'See how we preserve our papers?' he said. 'Millions of them! The passage of one thousand years couldn't harm a single paper we've preserved in here. We have numerous employees, but I rarely need them. I actually fired them all this evening. And now, N. A. ... N. A. Here!'

Alewi pulled out a large drawer full of files. But it was also full of other things he didn't expect. Plump cockroaches of different sizes shot out from between the papers. I saw at least two huge black scorpions crawl out one side of the drawer, and several shiny white lizards crept out as if they wanted to breathe some fresh air, which made me jump off the moving walkway in fear. In that moment I glimpsed several small yellow snakes raising their heads from between the files and swaying back and forth. Alewi was surprised and at a loss for what to do. He threw the paper, which had been in his hand the whole time, into the drawer's interior and shut it with a slam that resounded throughout the Archive like an exploding bomb.

He too jumped down from the moving walkway, took my arm, and rushed me back to the narrow elevator. He was infuriated, frustrated, and embarrassed, and he didn't say a thing. But as soon as we exited the elevator, he forced a disappointed smile on his lips.

'I'm afraid you got scared, doctor?' he asked.

I waited a beat.

'Not at all, Alewi, not at all,' I said.

'And now, to the Banquet Hall.'

'Banquet? Ah, I forgot!'

'Aha!' he called out after a short while. 'We made it!'

At the end of the passageway, there was an opulent, much-engraved set of double doors. He opened one of the lofty doors and gently pushed me inside, closing the door behind me.

Alone I shuffled into the great hall. In the middle of it lay an oblong table under an enormous chandelier blazing with light and crystal. Around the table sat about thirty men and women, all of whom stood up as soon as they saw me enter. A man in his late fifties with a formidable mien and gray hair called out from the head of the table:

'Welcome, doctor, welcome! Come over here, if you would. I've reserved a place for you on my right. We were worried about you, man. You're late!'

'Peace be upon you,' I said.

They returned the greeting.

'Here, here, on my right,' repeated the man at the head of the table.

Judging by his excitement and everyone else's solemn respect, it seemed I really was the guest of honor at the banquet. The table was set in a manner that bespoke the utmost taste and elegance, with bouquets of roses among the sparkling crystal glasses. Behind every few guests seated at the table stood a waiter in a white jacket, black pants, and white gloves. They really were waiting for me, for I had hardly taken my place in the seat of honor when the waiters began flitting about to fill our glasses with wine.

I didn't know a single one of those guests who had so worried about me and waited for me. Yet in my heart of hearts, I had reached the point where I was determined to proceed with them, and with anyone and everyone I met here, as if I really were the person they were expecting, or thought they were expecting. So then I would *be* Dr. Nimr Alwan or Adel al-Tibi, and I'd see what they wanted – if indeed they wanted something – from Nimr Alwan or Adel al-Tibi. It was clear that, wherever I came across these people, they preferred Nimr Alwan. Then I'd be Nimr, if only for one single, accursed night. I wondered, would they find me out and give me back my identity?

The host of the banquet turned to me with a glass in his hand.

'I hope you didn't encounter any difficulty on your way to us?' he said with excessive tenderness.

'I'll tell you,' I said, 'getting here was not easy.'

Concern etched itself over his features.

'Ah! Perhaps you came by the second way?' he asked. 'That's the problem with our location. There are two ways to get here. The first one's easy and direct. But the second? Oof.... The second is all ups and downs, twists and turns. I'm sorry, I'm really sorry, doctor. Anyway, the important thing is that you're here, finally, among us.'

'Thank God!' I said.

He sat up straight in his chair.

'Ladies and gentlemen,' he said in a raised voice, 'let's drink to Dr. Nimr Alwan!'

They all turned to me and raised their glasses in my direction.

'Here's to Dr. Nimr Alwan!' they said.

I drank my glass along with them, downing it all at once. I gestured to the waiter behind me to refill it. Then they brought the soup, followed by the fish, then the meat. Cups and plates followed each other with service befitting a banquet of such importance. That said, I was prepared to drink any drink, never mind that sumptuous red wine, and eat any morsel, never mind that delicious meal, after those long, miserable hours.

The atmosphere of revelry, diffused among us by the successive glasses of wine and plates of food, was clamorous. And I didn't know what exactly had brought those men and women of such disparate ages together in my honor.

Finally, the coffee was served, the cigar boxes made the rounds, and snifters of cognac were filled. Then the banquet's host brought his face close to mine.

'Are you ready to speak?' he asked.

His question shocked me.

'About what?' I asked.

'Just a few words from the guest of honor, doctor. It's absolutely necessary. And you're a master with words.'

I noticed the others turning their gazes – or rather, craning their necks – toward me. The host stood up.

'Ladies and gentlemen!' he said.

The clamor ceased, and silence reigned. He continued: 'A few words from our dear guest, Dr. Nimr Alwan.'

He took a piece of paper out of his breast pocket, put on his glasses, and began to read, his eyes flitting between the paper and his listeners' eyes. 'But before he gives his speech,' he said, 'allow me to speak for all of you in expressing the pride and delight we take in his presence among us tonight—the man famous for his strict adherence to seclusion in his house and his total indifference to making public appearances. We differ widely in our opinions and positions. We may agree with him, and we may not. And that's not only legitimate but necessary. Yet I think we can all agree that over nearly thirty years of continuous intellectual output, he has established for us customs, methods, and visions, all of which flow into a fruitful and productive stream that defines for us, in our tumultuous and blundering world, a clear identity from which tumult and blundering can take nothing away. Ever since I devoured his writings when I was twenty years old, I never for a day doubted that whoever confronts his or her own self thoughtfully, will ask himself that philosophical question which is the beginning and the end of all true knowledge: 'Who am I? Where am I going?' He has only to read Nimr Alwan, and he'll find the definitive answer, or at least, he'll delineate the landmarks that will guide him to the answer. That man who held his head high in the face of tempestuous winds, and was not shaken, and marched on, his eyes open to the future. Even more difficult, his eyes have been — and still are — open to the present in an age when we find that present ever more difficult to understand, ever more capable of igniting a burning anger.'

At this point, he put the piece of paper aside and looked at me as if he wanted to extemporize. Had he discovered the truth of my situation during our conversation? Did he now want to refrain from offering some prior analysis or praise he had prepared? The host smiled at me, then modified his sermonizing tone a great deal.

'Ladies and gentlemen,' he said, 'if you had had the opportunity to speak with our dear guest as I did this evening, you'd be truly astonished at his words. Do you know what Dr. Nimr Alwan told me just a few minutes ago? He said that when he regards himself today, he finds that he resembles a man who entered the Labyrinth by mistake, a man who failed to encounter the king's daughter at its entrance, as the hero did in the Greek myth. No maiden was there to give Dr. Nimr a thread to pull as he proceeded so that he would know – only after he'd penetrated the depths of the Labyrinth – how to return, how to exit for the open air.

'And if he *did* encounter the Minotaur at the end of the Labyrinth, he wouldn't know exactly what to do with him because he forgot to bring a sword. What can we say, then— we, hurled into the Labyrinth every single day with the Minotaur waiting to devour us one by one, for lunch and dinner; we, who weren't outfitted with the same keen blade nature bestowed on Nimr Alwan: the sword of a brilliant mind, which no monster or beast can withstand? Ladies and gentlemen, such is the humility of the learned.'

Humility indeed, Mr. Host, and what a trap you laid for me! I didn't recall saying anything to him about the Labyrinth or the Minotaur. How was I supposed to justify even a small portion of his eloquent digression? I hoped my head would split apart, cleave in two, to reveal someone unknown to me, someone who would rise to the level of that digression and pluck me out of my postprandial plight. I, who had forgotten my own name and my entire past, felt I'd descended to the bottom of my sieve-like memory to gather up any scraps that had defied the holes and not fallen through.

I noticed the guests clapping. Some of them clinked their glasses with their spoons and forks. The host, still standing, turned his gaze to me for the last time and announced: 'Ladies and gentlemen, Dr. Nimr Alwan.'

He applauded me encouragingly and sat down, continuing to clap. As for me, I took a deep breath, stood up, and heard myself say (as if the speaker were someone else!), hesitant and faltering at first, then gradually regaining my confidence: 'I really don't know how to begin, ladies and gentlemen. In ages past, our forefathers would commence speaking with a line of poetry which would inspire them with words that flowed effortlessly from their lips. But it seems that poetry − even though we still memorize some of it now and then − no longer inspires us with a new phrase or an important idea these days. The poets have said all they have to say, and listeners have heard all it's possible to hear, so there's no longer any poetry to excite anyone, even if it were recited. Despite that, some verses by al-Mutanabbi, ladies and gentlemen, echo in my mind and refuse to be forgotten—even by my memory. You surely know the lines:

'For every stalk of cane that time brings forth
A man is there to fix spearheads atop it.'

'Meditate on that with me, if you will. That stalk of cane, which the fullness of time brings forth to serve man and his noble endeavors on this earth in pursuit of the good— al-Mutanabbi sees, with his penetrating vision, that man instead exploits that stalk for the opposite of what nature intended. Man consecrates that cane stalk to accomplishing evil, to killing, and fixes a spearhead on top of it. To use the language of our time, al-Mutanabbi was a realist. He wasn't deceived by anything. He saw in humans that which impelled him to utter his famous phrase:

'To oppress is the lot of all souls, so if you find
A good, upstanding man, know that his vice is that he doesn't.'

'For al-Mutanabbi, the natural condition of the human soul is that it's tainted by oppression. Therefore, if a soul is too virtuous for oppression, that's because it contains a weakness, a hidden reason, that frightens it away from fulfilling what it was fashioned for. Man's goodness, then, his decency, is not a virtue. It's no wonder then that he'll fix a spearhead atop every stalk of cane that grows from the earth in order to kill people. However, let's continue with

123

al-Mutanabbi in his vision, with which he'll lead us to the matter that concerns us today:

> 'Every soul's desire? It is yet smaller than that souls
> should contend and expend with others over it,
>
> For youth will face down a scowling
> death but not humiliation'

'In these few words we find the lesson that Shakespeare's Hamlet will later learn, and for which he'll pay the ultimate price: Man's wish, his desire, his desideratum, however great, is still less significant than that he should be allowed to foment hostilities that could, in all their evil, lead to one of us exterminating, or *expending* the life of, another. Note the wordplay of the great poet in his choice of the word 'expend.' However, if the desires of others' souls lead to some kind of humiliation for the individual because he's too high and mighty in his virtue (and it would be more correct to say: in his vice and weakness)—the individual, in whose soul was originally planted the quality of oppression, just as the inclination to affix spearheads to the tip of every cane stalk was also planted in his soul—then, in that case, man must reject that false virtue. He must face down a scowling death and not rest content with any kind of humiliation.'

I stopped for a moment and passed my eyes over those sitting around me. All their gazes were directed toward me.

They had even put their wine glasses down. They expected more. So I resumed, as the smoke of cigars and cigarettes climbed slowly in the air:

'Tonight, this excellent wine of yours reminded me of other nights of mirth and joy, most of which happened in the distant days of my childhood, and perhaps your own, also very distant from us tonight. Nowadays, ladies and gentlemen, our nights are choked with blood. Behind that large door of yours, behind its two lofty panels, corpses are accumulating. Our fathers, our sons, our children, our women, they're being killed at every moment with systematic barbarity. At every moment, our houses are blown up, our cities burned.'

Surprise registered in the faces and eyes of my audience. It was clear that this was not what they were expecting to hear, al-Mutanabbi's verses aside. Yet they remained silent, gazing at me.

'Four or five days ago,' I continued, 'a friend of mine committed suicide to protest that barbarity. I didn't want him to commit suicide, for he was at the peak of his manhood, and I hoped he would continue raising his voice with us to confront the barbarity and killing and destruction. But he insisted that, life having become what it is now, death was a far better and nobler choice. I told him on more than one occasion, 'Don't let your despair become greater than you are.' 'Oh no,' he said, 'it's much greater than us all.'

'When I learned that he had actually committed suicide, I told him, addressing a corpse with a bullet-shattered skull—I told him, ladies and gentlemen: 'Your love for life was great, for when you discovered that life couldn't withstand all that love of yours, you rejected it. A world controlled by killers, lowlifes, and tricksters—you could not *but* reject it. And you were right. Your rejection of it was total, complete. You took your own life and put us all to shame.' The calamity shook me, ladies and gentlemen, and I imagined myself continuing my discussion with my dead friend. I told him, 'Like you, I too reject such a world. But until now, my rejection of it has failed to reach that towering climax which demands everything, which demands life itself.' The experience wasn't all that strange to me. Once, all my protest, rejection and anger had taken me to that line, as fine as a strand of hair, dividing life and death. And I nearly crossed it. However, an unknown wave, instead of sweeping me away into the clear, clean depths, roaring with their definitive silence, cast me back up onto a shore that was clamorous as well, but with depravity, crimes and deception. That was how I felt that day. But today, with my friend having finally gone silent, the report of the bullet he shattered his skull with still resounding around us, I feel I wasn't just lucky but extremely fortunate to return to that shore, raging with depravity and crime. Why? So I could confront it with my own will, with my head raised, with my eyes open, clinging to my vision from which tempestuous winds – as my dear colleague recently said

– would not shake me. And despite that, let me admit that I only came here tonight because I was forced to. And I came haltingly. If it had been in my power to refuse to come, then I would have, by God! That's because I ask myself insistently, why would you want *me* to be your guest of honor? In this world, so obsessed with its crimes, every day hurtling crazily from one bout of human slaughter to the next, what is it I can achieve for you such that you deem me eligible for such care, such concern? And what have *you* achieved in these bloody nights whose air is filled with screaming and howling, except to stick your fingers in your ears now and then and prepare yourselves a feast that may well be your last, and you none the wiser? Allow me to repeat myself, ladies and gentlemen. Behind that large door of yours, corpses are accumulating. And if you don't face up to the situation soon, then the corpses will spread out before you, here, on the floor of this great hall of yours.'

'Yes, yes!' the host shouted. I looked at him and found him shaking his head in pain, and tears – yes, tears! – flowed down his cheeks. I turned to the others, and suddenly they too were in tears, some of them wiping their faces with their fingertips.

'And I,' I yelled, 'I, who... I... I can be patient no more!'

'None of us, none of us can be patient anymore...'

I didn't know who had said that, but it sounded like he was choking back tears. I pushed back the chair behind me and set out resolutely toward the door while everyone was crying and heaving. The sound of wailing filled the hall. But a cry rang out, and it didn't seem to relate to what everybody else was going through: 'Come on, people! Is this how parties are supposed to end?' I heard someone else say, as I passed him on my way to the door: 'I don't think that's actually Nimr Alwan!'

As for me, I opened the towering door and went out, but before I could close it behind me, a woman caught up with me and closed it for me. She walked with me.

'I wasn't expecting all that!' she said.

I looked at her, shining in her beauty, her earrings, her radiant diamond necklace beaming upon her clavicles. There it was—she was my friend, my jailer, my manipulator. I was startled. Then I stopped walking.

'You! Again! Where were you?' I said.

She responded with astonishing innocence, one hand clutching her purse, the other holding a napkin with which she dried the last of her tears.

'Didn't you see me? I was at the table, not far from you. How did you find the group?'

She gestured with the napkin toward those whom we'd left in the room. When I continued on my way and didn't answer, she added, 'They're very sensitive. And very delicate. Right?'

'If their tears are any proof, like yours.'

'They're excellent actors.'

I didn't believe what I'd heard.

'Actors?' I said.

'Yes. A choice selection of the best actors in the land.'

'But Alewi said they were politicians and intellectuals.'

'Oh, you can call them that too. Anyway, the entire scene was filmed. Several cameras were in place, installed in different corners.'

I stopped walking again for a second, turned to face her, and grabbed her by the shoulders.

'Do you film everything that happens here?'

'Just about.'

'Then did you also film the drama between me and you in the Blue Room?'

She flung my hands from her shoulders powerfully.

'What scene?' she asked, pretending ignorance.

'Did you forget so fast? You and me, in the Blue Room, in the soft red light, and you in that sexy funereal dress...'

'God forgive you, doctor. I haven't been in the Blue Room in a long time.'

'You're lying!' I said with a mix of resolution and resentment. Yet she insisted on denying it.

'Not at all! Maybe there was another woman who claimed she was me? Or perhaps she claimed—'

'Exactly!' I interrupted her. 'She claimed that she... another woman... You too are an excellent actor. Just like the others. You're all great actors. And now, where will you take me? To the next scene in the script?'

Before walking me forward, she took my arm warmly and lowered her voice as if she feared someone would hear her, even in that abandoned passage. In her eyes was a look of endearment I hadn't expected from her.

'Listen. If not for me, you would now be in another place you can't even imagine. Believe me.'

'Ah, in that case I'd be executive-producing another film script, right?'

'Script? Okay. Go ahead.'

She opened her purse, put her napkin inside, took out a green card, and reviewed what was written on it. Then she put it back. We'd hardly got moving when she said, 'The exit form, have you filled it out?'

I put my hand in my pocket and took out the paper Alewi had thrust inside. I gave it to her.

She scrutinized it and laughed. 'All those names!'

'I hope they're to your liking?'

'But your name—you didn't write your own name on it.'

'Write it yourself,' I said indifferently. 'Fill in the blanks as you like.'

'All right.'

She put the form in her purse. Then she stopped while she lifted the purse's flap, the inside of which had a little mirror attached to it. She rearranged her hair, opened a powder case, and powdered her nose and under her eyes to remove the traces of tears. She took out some red lipstick and drew it rapidly over her lips. What's all this attention to her appearance about? I asked myself. Is it for my sake? Or for the sake of others she'll surprise me with in a just a few moments?

Chapter Six

She took me briskly through several doors and showed me into a sitting room she lit by flipping a switch. The room had comfortable-looking furniture and comfortable proportions, too. It was neither too big nor too small. For the first time I noticed that the walls were decorated with oil paintings of different styles, but all of them modern. Also, for the first time, my companion dealt with me like a housewife greeting a guest she respected. I wonder, did she finally believe I was Nimr Alwan? She invited me to sit down in a comfortable chair and offered me a cigarette from a case sitting on the glassy surface of an elegant coffee table. She took one for herself, which I lit for her using the marble cigarette lighter. Then I lit my own. I noticed that two books lay on the table, one of which my eyes suddenly fell on: *The Replacement*. I found that a good title for a book.

She'd hardly sat down in her chair to face me, taking a drag or two from her cigarette, when she said, 'Tell me, now, truthfully, what's your name? I mean, what's your *real* name?'

I was surprised at her question. I absolutely had to evade it because I'd given up trying to remember my name.

'Adel al-Tibi,' I said laughingly.

'No jokes, please.'

'Nimr Alwan.'

'Have you forgotten your name, or are you afraid to mention it? Don't you have some kind of ID card? Look in your pockets.'

'Stupid me!' I said, slapping my forehead with my palm. 'How did that thought not occur to me at the beginning of the night?'

I put my hand in my inside breast pocket and took out everything it contained: a small oblong notebook that contained telephone numbers and many blank pages, which I tore out every now and then to scribble notes or short messages on, and a shiny leather wallet where I usually kept my cash, ID, and business cards. I also kept some passport-sized photos of me in there, just in case. 'The problem's over, finally!' I said.

Yet what I found in my wallet was much more than I'd expected. As soon as I opened it, a bundle of cards and IDs of different shapes, sizes and colors cascaded from between my hands. Small personal photos were attached to some of them, as is the case with ID cards. Lamia (finally her name returned to me!) left her chair and stood next to me. Then she leaned over with her bare cleavage so that I could glimpse the roundness of her full breasts. She wanted to read for herself what was written on one of my cards, for I could lie or misrepresent things to her if she didn't see my name with her own two eyes. She even snatched the first card she saw from my hand and read: 'Dr. Fakhri Hassan Mansour, Orthopedist, University of Edinburgh.' Now we know who you are!'

A moment later she corrected herself: 'But the photo! That's not your photo.'

I offered her the second card, which was blue and folded. She opened it and read: '"Engineers' Union. Identity: Hafez Muwaffaq, Professional Engineer."'

'Look here,' I cried out. '"Ministry of Social Affairs. Ahmed al-Hashem. Occupation: Assistant to the Department Head." This card says: "Abdel-Noor Abdel-Ahad, Technical Supervisor". This other one says: "Ali Hussein Ali, Teacher, Al-Rasheed Secondary School". Hold on! This card's different altogether: "Mohsen Hantoush al-Shomali, Building Contractor". And here are three more.'

Lamia snatched the cards from me and began flipping through them. Then she let out one of her exquisite laughs:

'But the photo's the same! On every card, the same photo's repeated. Tell me, are you a professional forger?'

'Why not? Anything's possible.'

I scrutinized the repeated picture.

'Maybe this was an old picture of me,' I said, 'from, say, ten years ago?'

'Impossible! Where'd you get that wide nose from, and those thick lips? And the hair is totally different. Look in your wallet, and closely.'

I handed her the wallet. 'Empty it out yourself! You might at least find a photo of me in it.'

She took it and thrust her fingers into every one of its pockets. Nothing, except for a few loose bills.

She gave it back to me.

'Just as I thought,' she said, 'and thank God for that! It'll be my job to reveal your real name to you.'

I looked at her despairingly as she returned to her chair.

'I'm content with the name you honored me with tonight: Dr. Nimr Alwan.'

I returned the wallet and cards to my pocket.

'Do you know anything about him?' she asked.

'It seems he's an important person. And someone wrote a book about him called *The Known and the Unknown*.

She laughed as she exhaled cigarette smoke.

'That's just one of Azzam Spinks' inventions.'

'Maybe. Or one of Alewi's, the guy with the gold buttons? Listen, lady. It's late, as you can see.' I looked at my watch. 'It's past one-thirty. Don't you think it's time for me to leave?'

'Did you get sick of us that fast?'

'Did you say 'got sick of'? Are *you* talking about getting-sick-of? I'm certain that you all have brought me here because of some mistake—whether intentional or unintentional, I don't know.'

'Not at all. There wasn't any sort of mistake. In a little while I'll tell you who you are, so you can rest assured there was no mistake. And forget about those cards in your wallet.'

'Then you know who I am?'

'Of course.'

I found myself standing before her, pleading with her.

'Who am I? By all that's holy, who am I?'

'I'll tell you in a little while. Please, sit down while I make us some coffee. Would you like a little sugar?'

She said that as flirtatiously and seductively as she could. Then she stood up and headed toward a side door through which she left. Maybe it led to a kitchen. I returned to my seat as I stared at the door, waiting for that mysterious woman who, I was sure, took pleasure in her strange little game in a devious manner that I didn't understand. I was confident that she didn't know who I was or anything about me but that she liked to keep me susceptible to her seduction. Perhaps because, in doing so, there was a kind of confirmation of her charm, her ability to control a man whom she could impel to behave according to her whims, however and whenever she wanted. And she reminded me not of Souad – for whom I still harbored love, though that love had given her nothing more than a seven-year relationship, difficult and stormy – but of her friend, Yousra al-Mufti. When Yousra came into my life, I couldn't go two days without seeing or talking to her on the phone, even for a few minutes. That was a few years ago, when she thrust me into a tight circle of experience that shook the core of my being unto insanity. (Amazing! I'd begun to remember something of the past! But... I remembered Souad, and I remembered Yousra, but I couldn't remember my own name?) Yousra was then living the ripest years of her luscious femininity, which combined with a rare beauty in her face and physique that made men's – and women's – heads turn wherever she walked. She responded to the temptations that followed her about with increasing vehemence. And she had to – or so she thought – prove to herself that her beauty wasn't an illusion of hers and that her beauty, in attracting men, must also attract lovers who were absolutely infatuated with her, who behaved recklessly for her sake, and who whispered to her words of poetry. She responded to the temptation, if only a little. For, at the same time, she feared entanglement and attachment and took pains to avoid them. She rather delighted in capturing the care, attention, and infatuation of others more than she did in caring for them herself, giving them attention, or being infatuated with them. If she allowed a man to kiss her in a dark corner, she wouldn't necessarily crave him, of all men. If she bared her breasts for an admirer, or allowed his hand to creep up her thighs, she was really taking pleasure in herself, for herself. And in that moment, she almost knew the heights of pleasure without caring who caused it. For her, her beauty was a means of attracting a touch or a kiss that her imagination would follow through to the end, which she began demanding more and more. If she had the chance to be alone with a would-be lover, her first and greatest pleasure would be in seeing him stare transfixed at her body's beauty, and letting his face wallow like an animal's in the majesty of her belly or thighs. And if

136

he possessed her, or supposed he had, he wouldn't know she'd shut her eyes to him, or that she was wandering about in her own consciousness, which was closed to him, in the inferno of her isolated pleasure, her peculiar pleasure, which no one could share with her. She possessed *him* according to her own conditions, and wouldn't allow him, upon leaving her, to prize away any part of her essential self. Her lover might recall his pleasure at what he did. Yet what he did ended there. He wouldn't carry any of her affection, any of her longing, with him. He might discover that she'd used him as a means and not an end. And when she left him, she wouldn't take with her any bodily or emotional image of him except for her awareness of the sexual agitation she'd surrendered to in response to her unruly paroxysms, which she wanted to come again and again. And those paroxysms could recur within her until every part of her was deliciously and wearily spent. Then she'd surrender to a deep, dark, dreamless sleep. All that, I discovered for myself. And I suffered my pains for it. Then I went running back to my dearly beloved Souad, hoping she might save me.

I remembered that all very clearly. It occurred to me to be on guard lest the experience recur with this weird woman, Lamia, or Afra, after all these years. I reached for one of the two books on the table, the one whose title had enticed me when my eyes first fell on it as we entered: *The Replacement*. Pressed for time, for my dear companion would return with the coffee, I began paging through it distractedly. Suddenly my eye collided with a name that recurred throughout its pages: Yousra al-Mufti! Unbelievable! When I focused my attention on certain paragraphs, I found one that said, precisely:

When Yousra came into my life, I couldn't go two days without seeing or talking to her on the phone, even for a few minutes. That was a few years ago, when she thrust me into a tight circle of experience that shook the core of my being unto insanity. Yousra was then living the ripest years of her luscious femininity, which combined with a rare beauty in her face and physique that made men's — and women's — heads turn wherever she walked.

I was in shock. When I continued reading, I was overcome with terror, and my heart began beating with an oppressive speed. Did the book describe my experience – or was I in the midst of a gigantic trick my accursed memory was playing on me, recalling lines I'd read in a book somewhere—and then, I'd come to imagine that I'd composed the lines and served as the story's protagonist? *The Replacement*! Perhaps I'd read the book a few days ago and become familiar with its title. If that were the case, I had never in my life known a woman named Yousra al-Mufti. Then I was claiming for myself an experience I hadn't actually had except in the pages of a book I'd read. So I didn't remember an actual thing I'd ever done by myself! If I didn't remember the name that had accompanied me all my life, then how could I remember whatever else had fallen away from me with the passage of time and places?

Yet I couldn't be absolutely sure about my illusion. Maybe the deception was of a kind I hadn't even conceived of. Wasn't it likely, after all that had happened tonight, that that book was actually the story of my life? And how could that be so, unless I had written it? But I – and here's the tragedy – I didn't recall having ever written a book. Oof! I – who was I? I read books, but I didn't write them. I was the victim of a grievous mistake. Where was the old tart with her coffee? Where are you, Afra, Lamia, Souad, Yousra al-Mufti?

With all my strength, I hurled the book at the kitchen door, which I then went over to and violently shoved open, dead set on a final confrontation.

I saw a woman in a kitchenette about to pour coffee from a pot into four cups aligned on a silver tray. In my experience, a kitchenette usually adjoined a luxurious bedroom. And, indeed, there was a door in the opposing wall.

'You scared me to death!' yelled the woman, the pot quaking in her hand. 'What happened to you? Why don't you wait?'

'Are *you* here?' I screamed.

The woman standing before me was the other young lady, my accuser in the trial at the beginning of the night. She was wearing what looked like an official uniform: an orange skirt with an orange blouse, a small hat, also orange, that sat on the crown of her head and was angled down one side of her forehead.

Before she could answer, I exploded into words in which I could perceive only my anger and my sense of humiliation: 'I even forgot your name! Al-Saqi... Uh... al-Sa'ee... Haifa al-Sa'ee... Where's your friend? Where did she disappear to? And what is that ridiculous uniform you're wearing? Are you an airline hostess? Who are you pouring those four cups for? What's the meaning of leaving me alone to wait for coffee that won't come? And what's the meaning of this replacement, and Yousra al-Mufti, and Souad, and Alewi with the buttons?'

I choked on my words, empty of all meaning. Haifa was still gazing at me, frozen in place, the coffee pot sloshing its contents about from the tremor in her hand. She was so alarmed that she raised her other hand, its fingers tensed, as if to stave off a blow I would rain down on her face.

I screamed, my voice keen and shrill, and I hearing it as if it were another's. I wasn't in the habit of screaming like that at people, even when anger overcame me. 'Okay, okay, okay! Don't be afraid! I don't attack people. I don't beat women. What red hellscape did you come from?'

I must have seemed like a lunatic given my behavior and delirious screaming. I thought Haifa would throw the coffee in my face if I approached her. But she rapidly regained her composure. And not only that—she approached me and patted me gently on the cheek as she said: 'You've every right. You have every right to get angry . Everything has its limits. It's your right. Don't you want your coffee? Would you allow me to pour it for you? If you please...'

She went back to the four cups and began pouring a little in each one, one after another, until she filled them all. In the meantime, I watched her and got ahold of my nerves.

'The cream is gone,' she said. 'It must have splashed out of the pot...'

She raised her kohl-lined eyes to me slyly. 'It's your fault. You frightened me.'

Then she lifted the tray in her hands.

'Here,' she said, 'come with me. You're not the only one who's waiting.' She gave me a sweet little wink. 'Whatever happens,' she added, 'stay with me, okay? But first, open that door for me.'

'I've opened more doors tonight than I have in my entire life,' I grumbled. I opened it, expecting to see a fully furnished bedroom, with a wide bed, and perhaps a man stretched out on it, or a woman, or a man and a woman together. Who knew? Haifa passed before me, and I followed her.

Chapter Seven

When would I learn that I would always end up seeing that which I didn't expect? When would I learn to take things as they came, so as not to be taken aback by something new or surprising?

I did see a man stretched out, but not in a bed. He was stretched out on a dissection table. The room was an operating theater with powerful, dazzling lights. There was a surgeon in his long white coat, a scalpel in hand and a protective face mask covering his mouth. Near him stood a nurse – or was she a doctor? And who could she have been if not Afra, Lamia, Yousra al-Mufti? Despite her face mask and lab coat, I recognized her immediately.

There were also female nurses, not one of whom I could distinguish. And there were other doctors , and students. Finally, there was a tiered auditorium in whose rows sat a great number of male and female students following the surgical procedure, so it seemed, and scribbling in their notebooks.

Even though we entered the scene in total silence, all the eyes in the room zeroed in on us. Immediately, the surgeon raised his eyes in our direction, tossed the scalpel down, and pulled the mask off his mouth, just as he tossed away his cap that held in place his thick gray hair, and said warmly, 'Hello and welcome to our great thinker!' He stripped off his latex gloves and handed them to a nurse nearby.

Haifa then approached me with the tray, and I took a cup of coffee. She went over to the surgeon, who picked up his cup. She did the same for the female doctor, who likewise raised the mask off her lips and stripped off her gloves. As for the fourth cup, Haifa took it for herself and returned to my side as if keeping me in her care.

The surgeon was a man of around sixty, with strong features, white, bushy eyebrows, and ample hair, most of which had gone white. He was a lively and expressive image of the Wise Philosopher-Doctor as we imagine and wish to perceive him. He gestured to me with his hand, which held his coffee cup, and, in a high-pitched tone full of vim and vigor, said, 'Don't be surprised now, for once more you see before you Nimr Alwan, or Adel al-Tibi, or Alwan Adel, or al-Tibi al-Nimr.'

He took a sip from his cup. (I did too, urging myself to be patient and endure.) He continued: 'Not only are they all names for one man; they are all also, ultimately, as you shall see, one name – and no more – for a thing, a signified, divided perhaps into more than two parts who, one day, may or may not be mended back into one – he's the man you see laid out on the dissection table. The camera, please, so that it can illustrate the complete concordance between the face of the man on the table and the face of our esteemed guest.'

On a television screen on the wall before me, I saw a close-up of the man's face, then one of my own. Or rather, what the surgeon, or the camera, considered my face to be, because I, and I swear to God, didn't recognize either of the 'concordant' faces.

The surgeon-educator resumed: 'Perhaps you'll recall the French poet André Breton and his famous phrase, which he wrote in the days of his youth while in a dreamlike state: 'There is a man cut in two by the window.'

'As you all know, that formed the beginning of his theory about automatic writing, or spontaneous writing, which many of his peers later believed in and put into practice. Heed wisdom from the mouths of fools! Because that's what he and his fellow poets and painters wanted to be inspired by. They wanted to possess a kind of insanity that would simultaneously emphasize the wonder of human existence, its complexity, and how replete it is with everything our thinkers were unable to explain logically and definitively, even though all human civilizations practically emanate from it. That man cut in two, whom the French poet perceived in his window, is, rather, man as he attempts to see the two faces of his being and merge them: consciousness and the unconscious, reason and instinct, reality and dream-vision. And we could say that one of those two opposites – it would be more precise for us to say: one of those

144

antitheses – is standing before us right now. The other, who has materialized in a manner we'll attempt to explain at another time, is asleep on the operating table. Yet one contains the other. Each one of them is a half, and each one of them is a whole—at the same time. There's no need for me to remind you, as my colleague Dr. Lamia here will do shortly, that much of the creativity of not only painters and poets but scholars, too, in our age, as in ages long past – think of Sumer and Babel and Pharaonic Egypt – lies in the attempt to unleash the beast slumbering within. And I mean 'beast' in a figurative sense: it's a being very much alive, legendary and fabulous, very beautiful, very ugly. A being with a tremendous appetite, a tremendous lust for everything life contains, as long as blood flows in its veins. Therefore, much of the creative process, as I was saying, is an attempt to unleash the beast slumbering within, and at the same time, it is – and this is the key thing with respect to ourselves, living in a civilized society that adheres to reason and logic before anything else – it is an attempt to reconcile that beast (which is often difficult to control and extremely insistent in its demands) with civilized man, who lives with both eyes open to the real world, the tangible, physical world. The question remains: Is that reconciliation possible? And if it is, is it complete and absolute? What if discord ensues? What if the being, the essence, splits open yet again? Dr. Lamia, perhaps you could go ahead and respond to some of these questions.'

The Other Rooms

With the utmost delicacy and elegance, yet with a doctor's discipline and precision of movement, Lamia put her cup to the side, doing the same for the surgeon's, which she took from his hand, before approaching me and taking mine. She gave me a long, profound look. (Would she have been so concerned with collecting the cups if she hadn't wanted to get closer to me, to penetrate my depths with her wide eyes?) It's your fault, my doctor, my darling, I thought. Have you unleashed in me a slumbering beast, previously unknown to me? Yet it's a beast you've dominated, a beast you've defanged, a beast you've trained to eat from the palm of your hand! From the depths of my memory, cut in two, fragmented and fading, lines of poetry effervesced and shot forth like fountains: one thousand poems hurtled back and forth all at once from the folds of my brain, from the pores of my skin, and in all the world's languages I knew and didn't know. And I felt my lips moving with what I was inspired to tell her. I didn't exactly understand what I was saying:

> 'I caress all that you are
> And in all that remains, there you are
> I hear the incessant, melodious hissing
> Of your innumerable arms –
> A solitary viper alone among the trees.'

I noticed that the surgeon, Haifa, and the audience of doctors, nurses and students were regarding the solitary viper attentively, like me.

I didn't know whether I'd actually uttered what I thought I had. Yet I was sure she had not only intuited it but also heard it with her internal ear. It seemed she intended to face the camera lens (or lenses?) as she retreated from me and took her place near the head of the man stretched out on the operating table. She spoke with the voice of a lecturer confident in her expertise and directed her words to the audience, even though she trained most of her glances on me.

'Distinguished professor Dr. Ali al-Tawwab,' she began, addressing the surgeon. 'Sir, I submit that it wouldn't be farfetched to suggest that the mind of our great thinker, standing here before us, is now secretly overflowing with poetry. I also don't think it would be farfetched to suggest that most of that poetry is erotic, even though our guest, as far as I know, doesn't even write poetry. Perhaps that's part of the self's attempt to reconcile with itself, to reconcile the beast with the angel, the dream with reality, the impossible with the possible. If we were to infer a bit of what the mind of our friend abounds with – our friend stretched out here, the Other Dr. Nimr Alwan – then perhaps we might find it to be the opposite of what his alternative, replacement mind, standing over there, is currently thinking about...'

She raised her eyes to the ceiling. Her lips opened as if she were listening closely to a hidden, distant sound she was having difficulty distinguishing. Then she looked as if she were repeating it on behalf of the man stretched out before her:

'The full moon pours its light upon the threshing floors of
  autumn and
The shadows fall and fall again from atop the houses' roofs.
In their empty windows, Silence establishes his reign,
But between the roofbeams, rats emerge
Running back and forth, here and there, chattering...'

'*Nota bene*: silence, sadness, visions of childhood – nature, impassive, calm, and submissive, where nothing chatters save rats on threshing floors. Here we have peace and equanimity, here we have the sadness of the ages pouring forth like an old melody: 'The shadows fall and fall again from atop the houses' roofs / In their empty windows, Silence establishes his reign.''

Without warning, her tone changed. She turned to face me, pointing her finger as if accusing me: 'Doctor, what would you say if I commanded you to spill whatever's on your mind, instantly? Speak! Talk!'

I spun around. Suddenly, everyone wanted me to speak. There was nothing for me to do except choose a few words from the poems that continued to burst like fountains from the depths of my brain:

'A wasteland of thorns surrounds the city.
From the blood-soaked doorsteps
The moon gives chase to the terror-stricken women,
And from every gate pour ravenous wolves...'

148

I recited the words slowly, elongating the vowels as much as I could, giving weight to every phrase with the drama of misery and terror. But Lamia raised her right hand and yelled, 'Enough! Enough! My dear professor, he's evading! He's wearing another mask. Dr. Adel, put aside that mask of yours right now, for two or three minutes, and spill for us once again what's on your mind!'

I responded, involuntarily and unconsciously:

'Is it your eyes I love
Or your lips?
Is it your hands I adore
Or that slenderness in your figure?
Forgive this confusion of mine
For at times
It's your eyes I'm fond of
And at others, it's your figure,
All that's in you
Calls forth love
At first sight
And at first sight
Is adored.'

Despite what I'd expected given the formality of the occasion, or rather, its grimness, Dr. Lamia rushed toward me, her hand raised as she laughed and said, 'No, no! That's not what I meant!'

The Other Rooms

She looked around confusedly and maintained her laugh, which expressed her consternation, and perhaps her shame. But I was resolved to *spill what was on my mind*, just as she'd demanded. At that moment, the only thing on my mind were the words I'd just spoken. I knew her laughter could be a sign of protest, but it could also be a sign of satisfaction and acceptance.

'Your laugh, when it comes,
comes as a chime of madness for all who hear
stirring in the soul an echo
of pleasure
There's nothing in the world just like it
save the pleasure of my passion
for your eyes
and the pleasure of my longing
to encircle that slenderness
of your curved figure
which knows that it
sets fire to all
the blood in my body –
Or perhaps it doesn't?
Laugh, love doctor,
and sway, for my
eyes are fixed
on yours,
on your lips, on your hands, for

Every part of you God fashioned is
a wonder!'

The place erupted with applause. Even the great surgeon clapped. Not only did the students begin applauding in unison but they turned it into a rhythmical clap to express their admiration. They had no doubt enjoyed the fact that I'd addressed my amorous poetry toward their professor, as if I'd unleashed whatever was buried in their hearts for a female doctor they would have preferred as a lover and not a lecturer. I remained frozen in place, not knowing how to react toward it all. Be that as it may, I won't deny that I felt profoundly satisfied with myself!

But Lamia herself, however much she pretended otherwise, was no less satisfied by what I'd said, or less admiring. She waited until the wave of applause died down and silence reigned once again.

'We're in a state of extreme flux, from one extreme to another,' she said with total seriousness. 'And the speed of the fluctuation doesn't allow us to examine things with precision. Attitudes and positions grow farther and farther apart in those key spheres of life closest to man's experience in his day-to-day existence: he continuously tries to hold on to some fixed point, serene and tranquil, but the forces in motion keep acting and deprive him of any real serenity, any true tranquility. Our concern, as those who investigate reality in its many unknown forms, is to be able to check that motion when it reaches this or that furthest extreme and, in that moment of 'cessation,' once we've isolated it, to attempt to see what's actually happening in the mind, at the bottom of the human soul, where everything is important and momentous. If we were to ask this man in front of us, just as if we were to ask any one of ourselves: 'You—who are you?' – then he would respond, as a philosopher once did: 'As far as the universe is concerned, I'm nothing. As far as I'm concerned, I'm everything!''

'Dr. Lamia,' Dr. Ali al-Tawwab intervened, 'let me examine our friend Nimr Alwan. He may have begun regaining his consciousness before we accomplished our task.'

He leaned over to examine the features of the man stretched out on the table as I viewed the image of his face enlarged on the TV screen. It alternated with an image of what was alleged to be my face, and it bore a disturbing resemblance to the other image. Then the surgeon raised his head and ran his fingers through his abundant hair to replace the locks that had fallen across his forehead.

'Wonderful! Wonderful!' his voice rang out. 'I now remember a saying by the English writer – or was he Irish? – that stingingly satirical writer, Jonathan Swift: 'Life is a ridiculous tragedy, which is the worst kind of composition.' But whether life is a ridiculous tragedy or a tragic farce, we must get on with it, however badly it's composed. Or rather, we must accept the consequences of bad composition, with all the nobility and pride our spirits possess. This is what complicates things for us: Where's the tragedy here, and where's the farce? Which one of them makes us cry, and which one makes us laugh? Where do the two overlap, and why do they overlap? Moreover, if we were to examine the development we see in the life and thought of Nimr Alwan, we would see much of that overlap. In the space of twenty years, he has transformed from the rebel, the recusant, the provocateur into that which, from the beginning, had been intertwined with his formation: the teacher, the exegete, clothed in the mantle of prophecy, whether rightfully or not. He is transformed from the prodigal son into the hegemonic father. From the popular to the elite. And one often contains the other. Is there not, in all of that, the sign of a deep fissure in the self, that self in which opposites grapple with each other like the infidel with the believer, or the libertine who seeks nothing from this world besides his own pleasure, and the pious man who weeps for this world and strives only for the contentment of his Creator?'

He stopped for a moment as if he wanted the audience to contemplate sufficiently the depth of his wisdom and the wonders of his revelation. I didn't know if he was still talking about me, or about other people he'd thought up in the moment to justify a surgical operation, a kind of medical procedure I was unaware of. I was therefore delighted when Lamia interrupted him, at that very moment, with her characteristic skill:

'My dear professor, we must avoid oversimplification. We must grant ourselves the courage to penetrate to the densest and most dangerous of those dark corners inside the soul of which you spoke. If everything were countable, categorizable, understandable, then things would be easy. Yet the control of obscure dreams, only a small part of which we're conscious of when we sleep, remains in effect during our hours of wakefulness without our knowing it. And here's the difficulty: Those obscure dreams continue to foist the darkness and its ghosts upon us precisely where we seek the light and its shining visions. What I observe is that Adel al-Tibi, or Nimr Alwan — and let his name be something else entirely — has imposed himself precisely where his self no longer comprehends itself, where his memory has failed – the memory of experience – and of desire, where the only thing he has left is his instinctual reaction to everything he encounters, without the power to link anything with what precedes or follows it. In this case, what we anticipate is that his logic – if we can appropriately call it that – won't exceed mere delirium.'

No! That was more than I could stand. Even if I'd lost my memory, I wouldn't stand to be accused of losing my logic and reason as well. I interrupted the pretty doctor:

'You can all judge something that's the product of your imagination, while impelled by your own whims and fancies, and call it delirium. But I refuse for you to accuse me of being delirious. I only speak about what blazes within me, in my insides, where the fire is always burning, the fire whose flames I wish would spread in every direction.

154

Perhaps some of its heat, from the strength of the blaze, will reach you. Esteemed professors, dear students:

'If the clouds took up dust as they do water,
They would rain the blood of those we loved...'

'If you imagine there to be delirium in that phrase, then you're in an ordeal no one can save you from. I may be cut in two or into a thousand pieces. But I carry all the pieces and the fragments and the shards within me. And I know that even if I've lost my memory, I'll still speak of things you do and do not understand, drawing strength from the memories of many people gathered within me, just as the fragments and pieces are gathered. Who said they must be repaired and reunited, so long as they are there, present, active, struggling to ascend to the realm of light, to consciousness, uneasy and agitated, threatened in turn with falling into another sphere of darkness? Every memory within me is a burning coal covered with ash. There are many such coals, but how miserable! For there are even more ashes, many more. And for this reason, the miseries accumulate, and the pains pile up. My emotions, surging like the waves of the sea, are trapped within shells, like the djinn in Solomon's bottles. Trapped too are images wondrous and inconceivable. I might imagine that, if I shook my hands like so, the heavens – God's eternal heavens – would fall down from my fingers upon the earth, with men and women living in eternal love. But I also know that from these fingers of mine there might likewise fall miseries, follies, and sins. The abysses of hell could take the place of those heavens, and men and women would live in eternal torment. I passed through all of that tonight and on other long nights, in this room and in the other rooms I failed to find, such that I ended up saying what another man in another country and another era once said: 'Hell might afford my miseries a shelter.' Can a glorious angel break into hell to save a soul in torment from its blaze?'

'Now do you see what I mean?' Lamia yelled while facing the auditorium and pointing at me. 'His memory's broken down, his will is sapped. The only thing he has left is whatever shoots back and forth over the surface, like bubbles, with nothing to hold it fast, no axis to spin around. Yet these bubbles are still important and demand that we study them. This man – when he confuses or conflates heaven and hell – is merely confirming that his sense of logic has been shattered, that his sense of his sins and errors, whether real or imagined, is tearing him apart without giving up his yearning – which is also tearing him apart – for innocence, for purity, for that divine love that resides in certain parts of him, parts he can perceive using his senses and other parts he can't perceive. If we allowed him, even now, to expound and elaborate on his 'words,' we'd only hear so much more raving. And I won't deny that it could be a pleasant kind of raving to listen to. Rather, what's important is that, in his raving, evidence of many hidden meanings will be proven, as will indications of unknown obscurities we may hope to see or feel our way to, but which we won't grasp. We'll never grasp them.'

The surgeon interrupted her quite vehemently:

'Then what's the use of this operation of ours, Dr. Lamia, if we're going to claim in advance that we can't grasp the hidden meanings and the unknown obscurities? Don't you see you're harboring an element of futility, or, I could almost say, of despair, when it comes to an operation that depends precisely on counting, categorization, and microscopic examination in pursuit of understanding? Therefore, I'll now ask Dr. Nimr Alwan, or Adel al-Tibi, to approach the operating table after we remove his double, so that we can run more exams and tests on his brain.'

'No! No!' I screamed. 'You're all delusional! *You're* the ones who are stark raving mad! And that supposed double of mine, there on the operating table, is only a dummy you're trying to scare me with!'

I marched over to the man lying outstretched between the doctors and nurses and shoved Dr. Ali al-Tawwab aside so I could lean over the head they'd made in my likeness, certain it was a dummy or a plaster casting they'd sculpted and painted masterfully. I gripped the head with both my hands and shook it crudely, expecting it to separate from the body. But – how loathsome! – it opened its eyes and gazed at me. Then its arms moved. The body turned on its side feebly like someone waking up from anesthesia. The man stepped down off the operating table in a long white gown, despite the laboratory wires still attached to his temples and wrapped around his limbs.

'No, man!' the surgeon shouted, grabbing me to separate me from his victim. 'Come on! You've ruined everything!'

The victim, my poor doppelgänger, massaged his face and took off a delicate mask that he threw to the ground. I recognized him.

'Doctor Jassem!' I yelled.

He shook his head. 'Rassem,' he said, 'Rassem, Dr. Rassem Ezzat!'

It only remained for the surgeon, Dr. Ali al-Tawwab, to yank the toupée off his head with an angry, nervous gesture, his vast, sweat-soaked baldness radiating under the lights of the projector. Before he could strip off the thick, borrowed eyebrows too, I yelled at him, 'Alewi? I know it's you, Alewi! You did this to me! You did this to me, Alewi!'

I grabbed him by the collar and fixed my hands around his throat, wanting to strangle him. But he was tough and strong as a bull. He was able to pry my hands off him, push me away violently, and withdraw as lightly as a ghost before I realized I'd fallen between the arms of someone holding me from behind who, with the help of Rassem Ezzat, hurried me to the door. It was there that I realized the person holding me was Haifa al-Sa'ee, the flight attendant.

'Where's Lamia?' I asked her.

'Lamia?' she replied as if surprised at my question. 'She's gone. They're all gone. We're the only ones left here.'

'Where are the doctors? Where are the students?'

'Don't worry, don't worry,' said Dr. Rassem, trying to

reassure me, decked out in his loathsome white gown. 'You're in safe hands. Haifa, I'll leave Dr. Nimr with you. Give him a glass of water. I have to hurry off!'

He withdrew from us, seeming to run, and I ran after him, yelling, 'Don't forget to ask Alewi to send me a copy of *The Known and the Unknown*! Impostor! Conspirator!'

Like her female friend, Haifa was both extremely firm and gentle. She held me back so I wouldn't run after Rassem.

'What's with you and that poor man?' she asked. 'Let's leave him alone. Come on, we're almost done with the procedures.'

'Procedures? What procedures?'

'Don't you trust me?'

'Very much so! I have nothing but faith and confidence in you, in all those here, and in your plain honest dealing with me, all of you. Now you'll take me to Azzam Spinks, no doubt, because he's the one man we've had to do without in the last few hours, the man we all miss most...'

Her face at once filled with sadness. 'Have you heard, then?' she asked in a gloomy voice.

'Say it ain't so! He offed himself?'

'Enough with the sarcasm, doctor. He died. He died of a heart attack.'

'Awh, now you're gonna make me go and cry. For God's sake! Are you leading me up the garden path too? You're just another Lamia.'

She began guiding me into a well-lit tunnel. From the arched ceiling above us hung groups of colorful forms resembling ice crystals. They rotated slowly, diffusing light constantly.

'I'm not another Lamia,' my escort said. 'Remember that!'

'You're another snake in the garden—but a garden created by Satan, not God.'

'Have we gone back to raving?'

'I can only repeat: 'Hell might afford my miseries a shelter!''

'And what can I say about my own miseries?'

'Haifa, are you raving now too? Isn't one man cut in two enough for the two of us?'

'Ah, if you only knew!'

'Do you have something to tell me, then? Tell me, tell me!'

Maintaining her rapid walking pace, she said, 'So, until now you haven't figured out that I... that I'm not Haifa al-Sa'ee?'

'Amazing!'

'You won't believe me. I'm Yousra, Yousra al-Mufti.'

'You're Yousra!'

'Lamia blinded you so you couldn't see anyone but her.'

'But Yousra's not real. She's just a character in a novel, in a book.'

'You're still raving. What am I going to do with you?'

'I'll insist on my position this time. You *are* Haifa al-Sa'ee. But maybe you wish you were Yousra al-Mufti.'

'Me? I'm the most miserable woman on earth.'

'You mean for those you love?' I asked her in a voice not devoid of cruelty. 'Or for those who love you?' I immediately regretted my question and felt she didn't deserve my antagonism.

'I'm sorry, Haifa,' I said. 'But why are you, of all people, the most miserable woman on earth?'

She didn't respond. We kept speeding ahead until we reached an area where two other tunnels connected with ours. A throng of people poured forth, jostling each other, each one of them carrying one or more suitcases and hurrying toward the wide entrance hall we'd almost reached. It swelled with movement and resounded with noise.

'Where's your bag?' she asked, surprising me with her question.

'What about the bag?'

'Are you traveling without luggage?'

Then the situation revealed itself to me.

'Am I traveling?' I asked her. 'By plane?'

'This is a big hub, a train station. It's connected to the international airport.'

'Judging from that orange uniform of yours, you're going to get on the plane too, aren't you?'

'But which airline?'

'As if I know?! Is my ticket not with you?'

'I only have your exit papers.'

'Which Alewi arranged?'

'Along with Lamia.'

She took a few folded papers of different colors out of her breast pocket. She unfolded them and stood there examining them. Meanwhile, people passed us, rushing off, running, bumping into us, some of them apologizing, some of them not. Loudspeakers kept repeating information about the planes arriving and departing, and the names of those whose presence was requested at the information desk.

Chapter Eight

In the swelling mass of humanity, my attention was drawn to the face of a little girl in a white dress standing perplexed amid the crowd. She turned left and right as if looking for someone. And she held a red rose in her hand. I felt a strange sense of elation in that clamorous atmosphere as I continued gazing at the young girl's radiant face and glimpsed her wide, lustrous eyes in their constant, careful scrutiny of the people revolving about her. I don't think she was more than three or four years old.

'Look!' I called out to the flight attendant, pointing to the little girl. 'Look there—the most exquisite thing created by God!'

In that very instant, the little girl's eyes alighted on me as if she'd heard what I said. She appeared to recognize me and came running toward me through the human obstacles in her way. She offered the red rose to me.

'Uncle Fares! This rose is for you!' she said agitatedly as she panted.

'It's marvelous, just like you!' I exclaimed as I took the rose.

I lifted her up in my arms and kissed her on the cheek. She kissed me on mine.

'Wait here a minute, honey, with Auntie Haifa,' I told her as I put her back down, 'while I go buy you something you'll like.'

Without waiting for her permission, I hurried off to a perfume-and-candy shop on the other side of the hall and discovered that I had a few coins in my pocket. I hurriedly bought a collection of chocolate bars and bags of candy and returned with them to my kind greeter carrying the rose.

But she wasn't there. And neither was Haifa. People moved about incessantly. I began spinning this way and that, running among those traveling, those greeting arrivals, and those saying goodbye, scrutinizing every face, every build, every uniform. I didn't see the marvelous little girl, and I didn't see Haifa.

I felt a tremendous sense of loss the like of which I hadn't felt that whole night. My heart pounded with a painful intensity as I turned and revolved, the rose in one hand, the bag of sweets in the other, looking into every face, yet not seeing any face, not even seeing any human being. I wanted to cry.

A feminine voice over the loudspeakers shook me back to reality, saying, 'Mr. Fares al-Saqqar, Mr. Fares al-Saqqar, please present yourself at Information Desk Number Three...'

As by a roaring wave, I was overwhelmed by the feeling that the announcement was directed at me—me! I ran in search of Information Desk Number Three until I found it. I told the employee that I was Fares al-Saqqar.

'There was a man here looking for you,' she said gently.

A man wearing a black *thobe* in the style of the Gulf Arabs, along with a keffiyeh and an agal, approached me.

'Fares!' he cried as he embraced me. 'Welcome! I'm so glad you've arrived safely! But you're late, man! How was the trip? Relaxing, I hope?'

'It went all right,' I said.

'The car's waiting for you,' he said. 'Where are your bags?' he added.

'This time I came without any,' I said.

'No problem!' he said.

He took me by the arm, and we walked toward the exit. For whatever reason, I studied my new friend's profile. Then a passing thought arose, making me erupt with the question:

'Do you always wear a keffiyeh and an agal?'

He gave a hearty, throaty laugh. 'What else do you want me to wear with a *thobe*?' he asked. 'A fedora, or a top hat? Also, the keffiyeh hides my baldness, it covers it just so.'

At that, I forced him to a halt. 'Alewi!' I yelled in his face. 'You're Alewi!'

'Yes, Alewi Abd al-Tawwab,' he said, continuing to laugh loudly. 'Who do you want me to be? James Bond?'

For a second I was bewitched by a crazy hope. 'And is Dr. ... Lamia in the car?' I asked him.

'And who is Dr. Lamia exactly?' he said with an astonishment I hadn't expected from him.

'Pardon me, Alewi, pardon me!' I answered him, filled with disappointment. 'I'm just raving. For a second there I was afraid I actually *was* Dr. Nimr Alwan.'

'Doctor who?' he asked as we passed through the glass exit door. 'Why didn't you say John Jacob Jingleheimer Schmidt?' He burst out laughing with an excess of hilarity. 'That one, there,' he added, 'that's the car. The white Mercedes.'

He rushed me over to it. When I sat down in the passenger's seat and he took the wheel, it struck me that it was the same Mercedes I'd ridden in yesterday evening with Lamia. Or did I just wish that were the case, like someone wishing for the impossible? I lifted the rose and inhaled its dewy fragrance. At least this red rose was real.

When Alewi noticed my silence, he turned his head toward me and said:

'I see you're drifting off. Maybe you didn't sleep last night? Look alive! We've got a full day ahead of us. And remember, in the evening, you're to be the guest of honor at a dinner party the Intellectuals' Club is putting on at the Meridien Hotel.'

'You mean the party that's being held in my honor by a group of thinkers and politicians?' I asked.

'Yes, exactly,' he said. 'And they're going to ask you to sign copies of your book for them, dedications and all.'

'Which book?'

'What's wrong with you, man? Your book, *The Known and the Unknown*, the one you blew us all away with...'

'My book?' I cried out. '*The Known and the Unknown*?'

Alewi shook his head in despair. 'I don't know what's wrong with you! Unless you've now begun to get lost in the pages of your next book.'

'God forbid, man!' I said.

I gazed out the car's window toward the distant horizon. The sun had come up red and blazing amid wispy clouds that seemed to want to overtake it and catch its fire. And the sun rose toward an azure vast and endless, lush as a colossal rose, and the sky sparkled like lapis lazuli.

Baghdad

The Man Who Entered
the Labyrinth By Mistake

In 1968, Jabra Ibrahim Jabra toured five British universities, giving a lecture entitled "Modern Arabic Literature and the West." One of his central claims was that, just as the carnage of World War I had created a "feeling of cosmic catastrophe" in T. S. Eliot, who took the fragments of his self and transformed them into his epic poem "The Waste Land," so did the Palestinian Nakba represent a "universal tragedy" for the Arabs, whose world was in need of revival. The loss of Palestine in 1948 revealed to the Arabs their own kind of wasteland to be crossed if they were to enter modernity and claim their rightful place among the nations. As critics have argued, Jabra believed that for the Arab world to inoculate itself against further embarrassing defeats – such as the Arabs suffered to Israel in 1948, 1956, 1967 and would suffer again in 1973, 1982 and beyond – it would have to modernize. How? Both by casting off antiquated customs and traditions and by fostering a new civic culture that would lead to Arab strength and success. In other words, the key to establishing civil society and the rule of law in the Arab world lay in enabling the rise of a robust local culture of art and creativity. As a man of letters, Jabra did his part by making sure that change began with the word, with literature, and with education.

Forty years after the Nakba and twenty years after Jabra's lecture circuit in England, the Arab world would have just finished witnessing another, much bloodier wasteland experience. The 1980-1988 Iran-Iraq War was arguably as senseless as it was similar, tactically, to World War I. Chemical attacks, trench warfare, and massed assaults against fixed positions that resulted in staggering casualties evoked memories of Verdun and the Somme. Such attrition-style warfare accounted for around half a million Iraqi and Iranian combat deaths over eight years. Hollow men after the Nakba, Arab intellectuals were made hollower still when confronted with the carnage.

There were also traumas internal to Iraq that fostered an atmosphere of endless, uncrossable wasteland. In 1979, the head of Iraq's internal security services replaced his elder cousin as president by presenting him with a pre-written resignation letter and an offer he couldn't refuse. One of the first things Saddam Hussein did upon seizing power was to hold a snap meeting of senior Baath Party officials on 22 July 1979. During the meeting, Saddam sat behind a table on a stage and smoked a Cuban cigar while Muhyi Mash'hadi, the former president's secretary, publicly denounced other party members then sitting in the audience as conspirators against Saddam. Before the congress took place, however, Mash'hadi had been tortured and given a choice: either he would "confess" and denounce certain members as traitors or his interrogators would summon his wife and daughters, rape them in front of him, and then kill them. Mash'hadi chose to cooperate with Saddam in his purge. In total, sixty-six senior party members were escorted from the conference hall, and around one third of them were executed, by firing squad, by the remaining accused, most of whom did jail time after serving as the executioners of their former colleagues. The congress ended on an absurd note, with mortified party members raving at the top of their lungs about their love for Saddam, who they claimed was the only legitimate leader of Iraq. The entire event was filmed, and videotapes of the congress were widely distributed within Iraq and mailed to Iraqi embassies abroad. Saddam had set the tone for his rule—and for this novel. The same elements that animate that scene of absurdly theatrical politics make their way into *The Other Rooms*: the Cuban cigar, conference hall, stage, hidden cameras, politicians-as-actors, actors-as-politicians, automatic gunfire, and the neverending two-facedness required by a paranoid, murderous dictatorship that demands absolute loyalty. Indeed, the characters, events and props of that Baath Party Congress in 1979 so permeate this novel that Jabra could not but have been commenting on Saddam's Iraq.

The Other Rooms

The novel

The mid-1980s were some of Jabra's most prolific years. In 1986, when *The Other Rooms* came out, Jabra also published his translations of Shakespeare's *Othello*; Janet Dillon's study *Shakespeare and the Solitary Man*; and *Dry September and Other Stories*, Jabra's expansion of a previous translation he had done of English and American short stories. At the time, he was also presumably busy putting the finishing touches on *The First Well*, an autobiography of his childhood in Bethlehem that was to come out in 1987. The year 1986 also saw the publication of the Arabic translation of Jabra's study *The Grass Roots of Iraqi Art*, a fantastic volume that chronicles the development of modern art in Iraq alongside photographs and reproductions. The original English version had been published in London three years earlier. As for more original work, Jabra produced a collection of essays – *Art, Dream, Action* – in 1986, as well as *The Sun-King*, a screenplay about Nebuchadnezzar, the Babylonian king whom Saddam identified with, going so far as to rebuild the city of Babel and inscribe its bricks with his name, just as Nebuchadnezzar had done 2500 years earlier.

Among that incredible outpouring of creative work, *The Other Rooms* stands out for its absurdism. It's a Kafkaesque tale with resonances of Borges' forking paths and Sartre's *No Exit*. The novel makes reference to Greek myth (Theseus and the Minotaur), the automatic writing of surrealist godfather

André Breton, Chopin's *Nocturnes*, al-Mutanabbi's poetry, the work of English hymnodist William Cowper, Shakespeare's *The Tempest*, the English occultist Sir William Crookes, and the contemporary English poet Blake Morrison. *The Other Rooms* is written in the clipped and straightforward language of a hardboiled detective novel. And like a spy thriller, *The Other Rooms* is full of intrigue and mystery from the start, only the mystery is the identity of the main character. The closest thing to it that Jabra produced was arguably his translation of Samuel Beckett's *Waiting for Godot* into the Iraqi dialect in 1967.

As in Iraq in the 1980s, paranoia, crowds, executions, denunciations, and literal two-facedness permeate the narrative of *The Other Rooms*. Jabra's narrator does not know his name and cannot remember anything about his past. Is he Nimr Alwan, Adel al-Tibi, Fares al-Saqqar, or someone else entirely? The protagonist, who narrates from the first person, is inveigled into appearing at a government building, where he is interrogated by an urbane set of government officials about his identity. Who is he? What is his name? Who are his ancestors? What are their names? Their occupations? Everyone recognizes him and knows that he is a famous writer, addressing him with the honorific "doctor." His interrogators' mission is to determine who he really is, although they also claim to know already. They accuse him of evasion when he cannot give them any satisfactory answers. In contrast to Jabra's other novels, this protagonist does not drive the action but is driven by it, buffeted about by the whims of a massive bureaucratic surveillance state. Nothing is what it seems, and nobody knows who or what anybody else is.

Jabra's strange bedfellows

The questions "who are you?" and "what is your name?" were not exactly easy ones for Jabra to answer. Born in 1919 in the city of Adana, then located in the postwar French Mandate of Cilicia in what is today southern Turkey, his family fled the Turkish genocide of Assyrians in the early 1920s to settle in Bethlehem, then part of the British Mandate of Palestine. Jabra spent the formative years of his life in Palestine and considered himself a Palestinian through and through. Although he acknowledged his birthplace and birthdate on official forms and documents, Jabra studiously avoided mentioning his family history, place of birth, and emigration to Palestine in his role as a public intellectual. He also apparently studiously avoided correcting those who reasonably assumed that he had been born in the birthplace of Christ, given Bethlehem's symbolic resonances in his fiction and in world literature in general. The subterfuge outlived him as, until a few years ago, every single biography of Jabra began with some version of "he was born in Bethlehem."

Jabra fled the Palestinian-Israeli civil war in January 1948, four months before the Mandate expired. After making his way to Bethlehem, Amman, Damascus, and Beirut, the wandering Palestinian settled in Baghdad, where he made a living teaching at universities and teachers' training colleges. It was and remains no easy task determining how best to encapsulate Jabra's complex identity in a world as protean as the mid-twentieth-century Middle East. Was Jabra an Assyrian, a Syriac Orthodox Christian, a Palestinian, a Bethlehemite, a Jerusalemite? What about once he took Iraqi citizenship and converted to Sunni Islam? Why couldn't he be all of the above — and would the term "Arab" cover it? In an Arab world increasingly in thrall to the homogenizing forces of Arab nationalism and Islam as an antidote to centuries of decadence (or so goes the Arab nationalist narrative), would it not have been politically expedient to efface all the hyphenations of a complex identity to join what Jabra called the "great Arab civilizational flow"? I suspect that for purposes of simplicity and solidarity, and perhaps out of an aversion to the identitarian feathers it might ruffle, "Arab," "Muslim," "Palestinian" and "Iraqi" worked just fine for Jabra.

The name "Jabra Ibrahim Jabra" was, to an extent, chosen as well. Naming conventions in the Arab Middle East had not solidified when Jabra was born. The classic Arab tri- or quadripartite name – your given name followed by the given names of your two or three most recent male ancestors – was and is still used in many Arab countries, as it is in the bureaucratic police state of *The Other Rooms*. And while

the name "Jabra Ibrahim Jabra" has a certain ring to it –
like William Carlos Williams, Ford Madox Ford, or Gibran
Khalil Gibran – Jabra's grandfather's name was Gawriye,
the Assyrian form of the Arabic name Jabriyyah—not Jabra.
Jabra's Iraqi passport gives his great-grandfather's name
as Masoud. Jackie Jallo, a Syriac Orthodox woman from
Bethlehem whose family employed Jabra's father Ibrahim,
claims that the family's surname was Yahrin or Yaren,
although, to my knowledge, this has never been officially
documented. According to Syriac scholar George Kiraz,
it was not unusual for Syriac families in Bethlehem to use
Turkish nicknames or epithets – in Turkish, *yaren* means
"bosom-friend" – as clan markers in addition to their family's
surnames, which were sometimes lost to history. So, what was
Jabra's real name? Where was he from? Who was he? What
was he? The same questions are put to the amnesiac hero
of *The Other Rooms*. While other characters address him as
Nimr Alwan or Adel al-Tibi, even they are not sure that what
they're calling him is correct.

Scholars of Jabra's work tend to read his novels through an
autobiographical lens. As with the novels of Philip Roth, Junot
Díaz and Ibrahim al-Mazini, most of Jabra's protagonists
bear a striking resemblance to their creator: male, born to
a poor Christian family in Bethlehem and, at the time of
writing, comfortably ensconced in the Iraqi bourgeoisie,
which, as an outsider, he pillories even as he succeeds in
belonging to it. One could argue that it would be difficult to

read *The Other Rooms* autobiographically if the protagonist has no name, no memory, no known roots, no affiliations, no jobs, and no known relations and if he exists in a city and country that are also given no name and no temporal frame of reference. Yet I believe the novel is as autobiographical as all Jabra's others. The hero's relationship to the paranoid political entity that looks into every nook and niche of their activities and relationships properly characterizes the Iraqi citizen's relationship to Saddam's police state.

Jabra's name and origins were not the only facets of his identity that might have confused or upset the agents of Saddam's regime. From George Kiraz's recent memoir *Water the Willow Tree*, we know that as late as 1950, Jabra was a Freemason and a member of the Golden Throne Lodge (#1344) of East Jerusalem. A large number of Palestinian elites – Isa al-Isa, Khalil Baydas' son Henry, and a slew of Dajanis, Husseinis, Khatibs and Khalidis – were also members of the Golden Throne. The lodge was named for the regal seat of King Solomon, commonly regarded as the founder of the Masonic order for having constructed the Temple in Jerusalem. An Arabic-speaking lodge of the Scottish rite, the Golden Throne was founded in 1926 and boasted Jewish, Christian and Muslim members. It continued to convene under Jordanian and Israeli rule over East Jerusalem.

In Iraq, however, Freemasonry was linked to Zionism. In the same spirit of paranoia that produced *The Protocols of the Elders of Zion* in czarist Russia, the Baath Party conflated

Freemasonry with Zionism and, in 1975, made affiliation with either punishable by death. The Iraqi government clarified its position in 1976, asserting that the link between Zionism and Freemasonry had been "proven" and that the latter had been a "tool of imperialist and Zionist authorities." Indeed, bans on Freemasonry were issued and re-issued by Iraq's coupist governments in 1958, 1968, 1975, and 1976. In his book *Freemasonry in the Arab World*, Najdat Fathi Safwat claims to have viewed a list of Iraqi Freemasons in Baghdad compiled in 1958 that included prime ministers, doctors, military officers, lawyers, diplomats, PhD holders, and civil servants. We don't know whether Jabra's name was on that list or whether his affiliation with Freemasonry or the Golden Throne followed him to Baghdad, but we do know that the elite circles in which Jabra ran boasted plenty of Freemasons, current and former.

As noted above, affiliation with Zionism was punishable by death in Iraq. Bogus accusations of fifth-column support of Israel during the 1948 War had already led to the public execution by hanging of dozens of Iraqi Jews in the early 1950s, signaling the beginning of the end of Jewish life in Iraq. Saddam's uncle, Khairallah Tulfah, who helped raise the tyrant, penned a racist pamphlet entitled *Three Whom God Should Not Have Created: Persians, Jews and Flies* (1981), published toward the end of his tenure as mayor of Baghdad. Jabra certainly opposed Zionism. Zionist paramilitary organizations like the Irgun and Lehi had conducted nearly two decades' worth of terrorist attacks in Palestine during Jabra's childhood, blowing up cinemas and markets and assassinating competent, educated Palestinian leaders. Moreover, Jabra's family fled their home in the Jerusalem neighborhood of Katamon in response to the Semiramis Hotel bombing, which killed dozens of civilians and terrorized the neighborhood. Nevertheless, Jabra refused to engage in the crass and paranoid anti-Semitism so common in the Arab world. The archives of the Jerusalem YMCA, available online, attest to Jabra's cooperation with Jewish Jerusalemites in the various clubs and cultural activities of that iconic institution dedicated to fellowship and brotherhood. According to *The Last Jews of Baghdad*, a memoir by Iraqi-Israeli writer Nissim Rejwan, one of Jabra's first romantic relationships in Baghdad was with a Jewish girl, Evelyn Rubein. Along with 120,000 Jewish Iraqis, Evelyn was exiled from Iraq in the 1950s and moved to Israel, where she worked as a hotel receptionist in Jerusalem. Jabra also served as a mentor to young Jewish Iraqi writers like Rejwan and his circle of friends, which included Najib al-Manea, Buland al-Haydari and Adnan Raouf. Jabra's cordial, romantic and cooperative relationships with Jews in Palestine and Iraq and his affiliation with Freemasonry, innocent in their time, would have raised eyebrows under Saddam's regime.

Jabra might also have been a person of interest to the Iraqi Baathists because of his ideological goals. Jabra stated in interviews that he sought to achieve the modernization of the

179

Arab world through culture and, specifically, the written word. Jabra believed that this bottom-up approach – development through culture, as opposed to top-down policies of political, social and economic change dictated by centralized state planning – was the key to the Arab world's development, equality among the nations, and freedom to chart their own course. This could only be achieved through the right to free expression.

Coincidentally, the aim of modernization through culture was shared by another player on the world stage during the mid-twentieth century: the US Central Intelligence Agency. The CIA executed the policy of modernization through culture by founding front organizations such as the Congress for Cultural Freedom (CCF) and funding well-established philanthropic organizations like the Rockefeller and Ford foundations. These all supported the leading lights of Arabic literature in the 1950s and 1960s – Jabra Ibrahim Jabra, Nazik al-Mala'ikah, Tawfiq Sayigh, and Mounah al-Khoury, to name a few – with fellowships to obtain advanced degrees at British and American universities. John Marshall, associate director of the Rockefeller Foundation's Humanities division, helped Jabra secure a fellowship to study literary criticism at Harvard University from September 1952 to January 1954. According to Turkish historian Ali Erken, Marshall sought to identify in the Middle East a "creative minority" that would comprise the vanguard of humanistic change in traditional societies such as those of the Arab world. This elect could lead the "impregnable great majority" to the light. As Palestinian scholar Faysal Darraj writes in his book *The Novel of Progress and the Alienation of the Future*, this is precisely how Jabra saw himself: a "prophet-intellectual" leading the masses to proper values and true understanding. Moreover, John Marshall identified Iraq as the most meaningful ground for liberal, humanistic change in the region. Harvard's Widener Library holds a copy of Jabra's first novel, *Cry in a Long Night* (1955), with a personal dedication to John Marshall. According to Jabra's second autobiography, *Princesses' Street*, the sixteen-month Rockefeller fellowship made it possible for him to translate that work, originally written in English, to Arabic and begin his second novel in a room of his own at 60 Ellery Street in Cambridge, Massachusetts. Fellowships brought the aforementioned Tawfiq Sayigh and Mounah al-Khoury to live in the same building.

The Congress for Cultural Freedom also funded a range of cultural and literary journals during the Cold War, such as *Encounter, Black Orpheus, Mundo Nuevo* and *Transition*. The CCF's Arabic-language journal was *Hiwar*, which means "Dialogue." A Beiruti take on the *Paris Review*, it ran from 1962 to 1967 and published stories, novel excerpts, poems, and essays. *Hiwar* also published Arabic translations of essays by major thinkers of the non-communist left: Ignazio Silone, Denis de Rougemont, Robie Macauley, Melvin Lasky, George Plimpton, and François Bondy. During the Cold War, the CCF funded such magazines to turn the

Third World away from the Soviets' charms of universal proletarian brotherhood, which so often seemed to end in gulags, reeducation camps and killing fields. *Hiwar* was edited by Jabra's close friend Tawfiq Sayigh. The memoir of Arabic translator Denys Johnson-Davies, *Memories in Translation*, tells us that Denys and Jabra harbored "doubts" about *Hiwar* and never contributed to it. The pages of *Hiwar*, however, tell quite a different story. Jabra contributed numerous pieces to *Hiwar* from its very first issue in November 1962 until 1966, publishing two poems, three essays, three sections of his novel *The Ship* (1970), selections from Iraqi painter Jawad Salim's diaries, and at least two paintings. In fact, Jabra was one of the magazine's most loyal and enthusiastic contributors. An internal CCF report, held in the International Association for Cultural Freedom's archives at the University of Chicago, identifies Jabra as one of "the eminent personalities of the Arab world who have taken an active part in Congress activities."

In *The Other Rooms*, Jabra directly alludes to the literary debates that once raged in Cairo, Beirut and Baghdad. In those days, Sartre was *à la mode*, and the French Stalinist's notion of committed literature – his philosophy of inducing revolutionary social change through the proper kind of writing – found a receptive ear in Jabra's friend, the novelist and publisher Suhayl Idriss. In the first issue of the literary magazine *al-Adab* ("Literature") in 1953, Idriss writes that the committed literature of the Arab world will "spring from

Arab society and flow back into it," apparently throwing in his lot with Sartre. Nimr Alwan, or Adel al-Tibi, declares, riffing on Idriss' dictum, that *his true opinions* "spring from within and flow back in again."

In his introductory piece to this volume, Ahmed Saadawi reads this line as Jabra's implicit criticism of the "actual state of affairs in Iraq," in which one kept one's private opinions to oneself. Yet one could also read the line as proof that Jabra continued to occupy the anti-ideological side of the debate about literature's place in society more than thirty years after that debate's first salvos in the pages of *al-Adab*. Jabra was an introspective writer, and understanding his true opinions, his self, and his interior was his lifelong project. Improving Arab society may have been Jabra's long-term goal, yet he sought to do so not by writing political literature burdened with ideological commitment but by creating art and literature that focused intensely on the undulations of the human soul.

Another way the CCF sought to steer the ship of Arab culture through the Cultural Cold War was through conferences. At the Rome Conference, held in October 1961 at the tony Hermitage Hotel, Jabra gave a paper entitled *The Short Story, the Novel and the Theater: Their Role in Arab Society and Their Future in Relation to Foreign Literature*. In Rome, Jabra met the conference's organizer and attendee, John Clinton Hunt. Hunt was a novelist, a CIA officer and a Harvard alumnus who ran the CCF's operations out of Paris. True to his surname, Hunt chased down third-world literary talent

183

to found magazines that would support the ideas of the non-communist left in the same way that Marshall targeted Arab intellectuals and writers for generous Rockefeller grants. It was Hunt who approached Johnson-Davies about the Arabic literary magazine that would become *Hiwar*. At the 1961 Rome Conference, which scholar of Arabic literature Robyn Creswell has referred to as an "audition" for the Arab literary modernists to start a magazine, Hunt sought to identify an Arab intellectual who could best serve as the editor of the literary journal the CCF would soon establish and fund.

In addition to Hunt and Marshall, Jabra also knew an American named William Roe Polk. A protégé of John Marshall, Bill Polk would become one of the US's premier postwar Arabists, going on to work for the US State Department and to lead the University of Chicago's Middle East Studies program. As an undergraduate at Harvard, Polk spent the summer of 1950 traveling in Cairo, Baghdad and Beirut to research local students' organizations for the US National Student Association. The research Polk conducted that summer became his senior thesis, which helped him win a Rockefeller Foundation Fellowship after graduation. He would be awarded three more during his life. According to Polk's autobiography, *Personal History*, he then became the mentee of John Marshall for the next few years. He also moved to Baghdad, where he was able to observe Iraqi society from within, avoided the expatriate crowd, and devoted himself to learning Arabic and traveling the country. According to

Middle East historian Nathan Citino, Polk was in the habit of hosting salon-style political discussions at his apartment. He befriended Jabra's friends – the poet Nazik al-Mala'ikah and historian Abd al-Aziz al-Duri – and produced a booklet called *What the Arabs Think*. Though Polk missed Jabra at Harvard by a few months, his surviving daughter Milbry has passed on to me that Polk's diary records his meeting Jabra along with British Orientalist Sir Hamilton A. R. Gibb in 1952, 1953, and 1954. Amusingly, Jabra is listed in Polk's address book as "very, very English." Indeed, linking Jabra, Polk, and Marshall was Gibb, who taught at Harvard from 1955 to 1964 and served as the director of Harvard's Center for Middle Eastern Studies. Before he went to Harvard, Gibb trained Polk in Arabic at Oxford in an academic mentorship set up by Marshall, who sought to cultivate American Arabists for a country that largely lacked them. To follow the trail of Jabra's dedications, Widener Library's copy of Jabra's short story collection, *Sweet and Other Stories* (1956), is dedicated, in Jabra's hand, to "the great scholar Sir Hamilton Gibb, with my profound admiration for his thought."

Once we begin drawing connections between the CIA, the CCF, the Rockefeller Foundation, and their Arab beneficiaries, a vast network of creative writers, translators, conference coordinators, financial enablers, scholarship recipients, intelligence officers, and philologists appears, much like it did in other parts of the world following the *New York Times'* revelation in 1966 that the CCF was funded by the CIA. The question ceases to be whether these men and women collaborated with each other and instead becomes to what extent Arab writers were aware that they were collaborating with the CIA because of their shared liberal, humanist commitment to the freedom of expression and modernization through culture. One also wonders what modern Arabic literature would have become without the covert nourishment provided by the CIA.

Interestingly, Jabra's involvement with liberal American institutions was a continuation of his sponsorship by a similar British one from 1939-1943. The United Kingdom's premier overseas cultural-diplomatic organization, the British Council was founded in 1934 to compete with similar Soviet, Italian, and French propaganda initiatives. As the file on Jabra in the Fitzwilliam House archives makes clear, the British Council funded a year of Jabra's study at Exeter so that Jabra would return to Palestine one year later a better teacher and disseminator of British values. As the war intensified, Jabra cited fears of returning to Palestine by boat during wartime. He stayed on in England, transferring to Fitzwilliam House at Cambridge University and extending his scholarship year by year until he took a degree. The British Council offered these scholarships not only to spread British cultural values and harvest a crop of teachers for the Palestine Government's schools but also to ensure that, when the Mandate expired, the former colonies would have enough know-how to govern themselves and participate on the world stage. The men and women who managed Jabra's scholarship were themselves major players in education and empire: Ifor Evans, professor and university administrator; Douglas Parmée, secretary to the students' committee at the British Council; William Sutherland Thatcher, Censor of Fitzwilliam House; Jerome Farrell, the British Colonial Office's director of education; Philip Cox of the Colonial Office; John Murray, principal of the University College of the South West, Exeter; Helena Mennie Shire, Jabra's tutor at Cambridge; and H. L. Thornton, Director of Colonial Scholars. The British Council's file on him brims with their correspondence with and about Jabra Ibrahim Jabra, whom Shire describes as a "very intelligent and gifted student, with a special flair for literary expression and appreciation." Thatcher described him as "honest and industrious," and a "pleasant person to work with." From the hindsight of one hundred years, a pattern begins to emerge of the Anglo-American powers projecting influence, over decades, through the cultivation of intellectuals like Jabra.

The fact that Jabra knew and worked with these key actors and organizations is not necessarily suspicious. The ideas of the non-communist left were in the cultural water that everyone drank, and the intellectual circles of Jabra's Baghdad were no exception. Whether Jabra was a witting collaborator of the US in the Cultural Cold War is not known to me. But he was a vigorous supporter of goals that the US too then held dear. It would be hasty to interpret Jabra's affiliations and relationships as evidence that he was a stooge of colonial powers or that his efforts to achieve the social, economic, scientific, military and political advancement of the Arab world through cultural modernization were insincere. My contention here is that Jabra may have had cause for worry in Saddam's Iraq, where merely having associated with such organizations could lead to accusations, torture, a show trial, and execution. Jabra's involvement with Freemasonry, Iraqi Jewish intellectuals, and key players in the Cultural Cold War should not send us down a conspiratorial rabbit hole. Yet if I were a counterintelligence investigator in a security state as paranoid as Saddam's, I would be very interested in Jabra, his affiliations, his personal relationships, his cultural activities, his frequent trips abroad, and his murky family backstory.

How are all these facts relevant to *The Other Rooms*? They account for the sense of predation that pervades the novel. The hero's interrogators are constantly probing into his past to find out who he really is, as if a hermeneutic essence lies forever beyond their reach. Their search for his identity drives the action of the novel. To be sure, uncovering the true identity of the hero is not a new theme for Jabra. *In Search of Walid Masoud* (1978), Jabra's fourth novel, revolves around a group of bourgeois Iraqis attempting to reconstruct the identity of their friend Walid, who has fled and left clues behind. What is new about the investigation into the hero's identity in *The Other Rooms* is that the search is conducted by the interrogators of the state's security services, who are convinced that the protagonist is hiding something about his identity. And his identity is as opaque as their questions are relentless.

Jabra and Saddam

It's difficult to square the image of Jabra that appeared later in life with his younger self. Superficially at least, the onetime champion of cultural freedom seemed to have turned into a fervid supporter of Saddam Hussein. In Jeff B. Harmon's documentary film *Saddam's Iraq*, filmed just weeks before the First Gulf War broke out in 1991, Jabra claims that he regards Saddam with an "admiration that goes beyond love." When Harmon asks him whether he would be willing to die for Saddam, Jabra responds with a question: "Would I die for a man who has been responsible for the great progress of this country? I would die for anyone who makes possible the independence and dignity of this nation. And he has made it possible." Harmon confronts Jabra with the fact that the ubiquitous pictures of Saddam in Iraq's public and private spaces remind the filmmaker of a personality cult. But Jabra characterizes the likenesses as an eminently reasonable explanation for the

> 'popularity of the president. He is very popular. Now there is a man who comes up from the soil of the country, who is part of the people, who speaks their language and

yet who actually gives them a sense of pride and dignity and makes work possible, everything, makes education free for everybody. I think it is very natural that he has achieved the popularity that would make them want to hang his picture everywhere... Nobody compels you to put a picture in your room if you don't want to. But who knows what is in the hearts of men. I mean, Shakespeare complained about it, didn't he? But if there is so much love, surely a lot of it has to be sincere.'

Jabra sounds reasonable, sincere and convincing. Yet one also senses that he is reaching for diplomatic answers that will neither sully his reputation as an independent thinker nor get him killed. A representative of the Iraqi state was attached to Harmon and his filming crew and sat in on Harmon's interviews, so Jabra's expressed sentiments may have been forced. They may also have been sincere, at least to some extent. Saddam devoted the state's resources to combating illiteracy, educating women, providing free healthcare for Iraqis, and granting Palestinian refugees the rights and privileges accorded to native-born Iraqis. Given the limits on free expression in Iraq at the time, it may be impossible to know how Jabra really felt about Saddam Hussein.

Staying alive and staying put

Why didn't Jabra leave Iraq? Jabra had money, friends, and family abroad. Since Jabra's arrival there in 1948, Iraq had devolved, one coup after another, into a failed state governed by a genocidal tyrant, crippled by UN sanctions, and threatened by simmering internecine strife from within and Western military might from without. One wonders whether Jabra did not decide to remain in the failed state that Iraq had become because he had tired of fleeing. Even before he was born, Jabra was prey. His parents Ibrahim and Maryam survived the Assyrian genocide, the Sayfo, before he was born. Staying in the newly created state of Turkey would probably have meant death for him, as it did for thousands of Assyrian, Greek, and Armenian Christians exposed to the ravages of Ataturk's army after the French withdrawal from Adana in 1922. In 1948, staying in Jerusalem may have meant death for him, too, as Zionist militias went about blowing up houses and terrorizing the non-Jewish families of Katamon to induce them to flee. I wonder if Jabra didn't leave Iraq because, the third time around, he was determined to die at his post rather than flee again. Perhaps he decided to dig in and improve the position he had established for himself over the past forty years. When the hero of *The Other Rooms* is told he is a victim and absolved of responsibility for his actions, he responds angrily, saying, "What kind of lying nonsense is this? ... I absolutely reject what you're claiming. I'm not the victim of anything or anybody." Perhaps Jabra, like Nimr Alwan, refused to be a victim.

One element of *The Other Rooms* that harmonizes with Jabra's other novels is suicide. The forlorn hero of *Cry in a Long Night*, Amin Samma, rejects the idea of suicide by recalling a folktale his father once told him. Two characters in Jabra's novel *The Ship* kill themselves while the novel's characters debate suicide's usefulness. Walid Masoud from the eponymous novel effectively effaces himself, leaving his car at the Rutba border crossing with Syria and disappearing into the desert. But the protagonist in *The Other Rooms*, like Jabra's character Amin, rejects suicide. During the novel's banquet scene, Nimr Alwan recounts that one of his friends had contemplated suicide, debated it, and then finally committed it. Nimr claims to understand and respect his friend's choice, but he decides against it for himself. Why?

'Once, all my protest, rejection and anger had taken me to that line, as fine as a strand of hair, dividing life and death. And I nearly crossed it. However, an unknown wave, instead of sweeping me away into the clear, clean depths, roaring with their definitive silence, cast me back up onto a shore that was clamorous as well, but with depravity, crimes and deception. That was how I felt that day. But today, with my friend having finally gone silent, the report of the bullet he shattered his skull with still resounding around us, I feel

I wasn't just lucky but extremely fortunate to return to that shore, raging with depravity and crime. Why? So I could confront it with my own will, with my head raised, with my eyes open, clinging to my vision from which tempestuous winds – as my dear colleague recently said – would not shake me.'

As the translator of Germaine Brée's biography of Albert Camus, Jabra would have been familiar with the *Sisyphus* essay and Camus' rejection of self-murder. Like Sisyphus, Nimr Alwan, Adel al-Tibi, or Fares al-Saqqar, their author and creator Jabra Ibrahim Jabra refused to go silent and refused to budge, choosing to remain in a surrealist Iraq with his head raised, his eyes open, confronting its absurdity with his will and clinging to his vision of the Arab future. Whether he succeeded or failed, nothing shook him from his course. One must imagine Jabra happy.

William Tamplin